LEFT

TO

MURDER

(An Adele Sharp Mystery—Book Five)

BLAKE PIERCE

Blake Pierce

Blake Pierce is the USA Today bestselling author of the RILEY PAGE mystery series, which includes seventeen books. Blake Pierce is also the author of the MACKENZIE WHITE mystery series, comprising fourteen books; of the AVERY BLACK mystery series, comprising six books; of the KERI LOCKE mystery series, comprising five books; of the MAKING OF RILEY PAIGE mystery series, comprising six books; of the KATE WISE mystery series, comprising seven books; of the CHLOE FINE psychological suspense mystery, comprising six books; of the JESSE HUNT psychological suspense thriller series, comprising fourteen books (and counting); of the AU PAIR psychological suspense thriller series, comprising three books; of the ZOE PRIME mystery series, comprising four books (and counting); of the new ADELE SHARP mystery series, comprising six books (and counting); of the new EUROPEAN VOYAGE cozy mystery series, comprising six books (and counting); and of the new LAURA FROST FBI suspense thriller.

An avid reader and lifelong fan of the mystery and thriller genres, Blake loves to hear from you, so please feel free to visit www.blakepierceauthor.com to learn more and stay in touch.

ISBN: 9781094350233

BOOKS BY BLAKE PIERCE

LAURA FROST FBI SUSPENSE THRILLER
ALREADY GONE (Book #1)
ALREADY SEEN (Book #2)
ALREADY TRAPPED (Book #3)

EUROPEAN VOYAGE COZY MYSTERY SERIES
MURDER (AND BAKLAVA) (Book #1)
DEATH (AND APPLE STRUDEL) (Book #2)
CRIME (AND LAGER) (Book #3)
MISFORTUNE (AND GOUDA) (Book #4)
CALAMITY (AND A DANISH) (Book #5)
MAYHEM (AND HERRING) (Book #6)

ADELE SHARP MYSTERY SERIES
LEFT TO DIE (Book #1)
LEFT TO RUN (Book #2)
LEFT TO HIDE (Book #3)
LEFT TO KILL (Book #4)
LEFT TO MURDER (Book #5)
LEFT TO ENVY (Book #6)
LEFT TO LAPSE (Book #7)

THE AU PAIR SERIES
ALMOST GONE (Book#1)
ALMOST LOST (Book #2)
ALMOST DEAD (Book #3)

ZOE PRIME MYSTERY SERIES
FACE OF DEATH (Book#1)
FACE OF MURDER (Book #2)
FACE OF FEAR (Book #3)
FACE OF MADNESS (Book #4)
FACE OF FURY (Book #5)
FACE OF DARKNESS (Book #6)

A JESSIE HUNT PSYCHOLOGICAL SUSPENSE SERIES
THE PERFECT WIFE (Book #1)
THE PERFECT BLOCK (Book #2)
THE PERFECT HOUSE (Book #3)
THE PERFECT SMILE (Book #4)
THE PERFECT LIE (Book #5)
THE PERFECT LOOK (Book #6)
THE PERFECT AFFAIR (Book #7)
THE PERFECT ALIBI (Book #8)
THE PERFECT NEIGHBOR (Book #9)
THE PERFECT DISGUISE (Book #10)
THE PERFECT SECRET (Book #11)
THE PERFECT FAÇADE (Book #12)
THE PERFECT IMPRESSION (Book #13)
THE PERFECT DECEIT (Book #14)
THE PERFECT MISTRESS (Book #15)

CHLOE FINE PSYCHOLOGICAL SUSPENSE SERIES
NEXT DOOR (Book #1)
A NEIGHBOR'S LIE (Book #2)
CUL DE SAC (Book #3)
SILENT NEIGHBOR (Book #4)
HOMECOMING (Book #5)
TINTED WINDOWS (Book #6)

KATE WISE MYSTERY SERIES
IF SHE KNEW (Book #1)
IF SHE SAW (Book #2)
IF SHE RAN (Book #3)
IF SHE HID (Book #4)
IF SHE FLED (Book #5)
IF SHE FEARED (Book #6)
IF SHE HEARD (Book #7)

THE MAKING OF RILEY PAIGE SERIES
WATCHING (Book #1)
WAITING (Book #2)
LURING (Book #3)
TAKING (Book #4)
STALKING (Book #5)
KILLING (Book #6)

CAUSE TO SAVE (Book #5)
CAUSE TO DREAD (Book #6)

KERI LOCKE MYSTERY SERIES
A TRACE OF DEATH (Book #1)
A TRACE OF MUDER (Book #2)
A TRACE OF VICE (Book #3)
A TRACE OF CRIME (Book #4)
A TRACE OF HOPE (Book #5)

CHAPTER ONE

A lonely ray of light refracted through the violet liquid in the bulbous glass, casting a purplish sheen across the naked table. Streaks of azure formed in the blue stone swirls of the circular surface, and Amelia Gueyen wiped down the table, retrieving the remaining glass and placing it on the brown tray resting askew across the backrests of two cushioned chairs.

She arched her back, wincing against a small twinge, before balancing the tray of half-sipped wine glasses and returning to the crisscrossing wooden display case behind the carved oak counter. She sighed, tipping the contents of the glasses into the metal sink hidden behind the counter's oak frame, before placing the delicate crystal in the plastic wash-holder. One of the openers tomorrow would slot the things into the economy-sized dishwasher before the first customers arrived. She hoped they would remember to leave the settings on *low* this time. She didn't want it to be like last time, where she had to clean up a fiasco of shattered glass pieces scattered throughout the most expensive appliance in the place.

She felt another twinge and half-turned, shifting uncomfortably in her white and black uniform. Swirling gold and blue letters spelled the name *Chateau Bordeaux* across her lapel, next to the small golden badge that bore the letters GUEYEN.

She glanced toward the dipping sun through the glass windows set in the far wall of the wine-tasting studio. She blinked a couple of times against the sparkles of light tiptoeing through the veiled glass. Evening was quickly approaching. She glanced at her watch. *4:23.*

Nearly half an hour after they'd closed.

So why was there still a gray sedan in the far parking space behind the dumpsters? She frowned and tilted her head, staring behind the counter that led into the kitchens. "Andre?" she called, raising her voice. "Andre, are you here?"

No answer.

She wrinkled her nose. She gently pushed the wooden tray, making sure it was stable on the counter, before dusting off her hands and

1

moving with swift steps through the room toward the glass window. She didn't recognize the gray car—nor did she know any of the employees silly enough to park so close to the dumpsters.

"Andre?" she called again, raising her voice.

Sometimes the older sommelier would stop by during Amelia Gueyen's hours. She never appreciated these surprise visits—and it often felt like the older man looked over her shoulder during every movement, as if judging her words or behavior.

While it was true she'd only been working as a sommelier for the last year, she'd spent enough time in study, along with growing up on her grandfather's own vineyard, that she was happy to test her knowledge and palate against the best wine-tasters in the game.

The last group of tourists who'd passed through certainly hadn't seemed to have any complaints. Especially not the last bearded fellow with the belly—he'd tried to slide her his number in his glass. She'd tossed the contents in the sink while he'd watched from across the room. His look of dejection hadn't pleased her, but one could only stomach so much unsolicited attention before exhaustion set in. Sparing feelings was not why Amelia had signed up for this job—grapes didn't have feelings, and fermentation was a slow, careful art, but also a science. A sommelier's job, combined with the vineyard, was the perfect marriage of science and art in Amelia Gueyen's estimation.

She reached the window now, peering out into the parking lot beyond the wine-tasting studio. For a moment, she felt a flicker of fear. What if the car belonged to the bearded fellow? Maybe he'd been embarrassed in front of his friends when she'd tossed the note.

Maybe he wanted to have a word. Maybe more...

She shivered and quickly hurried to the door, ignoring the twinge in her back from over-lifting a carton earlier that day. She moved toward the lock, but just then, the small tinkling chimes above the door rattled quietly, emitting a soft, musical series of notes.

And the door creaked open, slowly, with the eerie motion of a coffin lid sliding ajar.

Amelia stiffened, staring at the door, one hand half-extended, the other massaging her lower back. Her eyes darted to the wooden tray she'd left on the counter. She could feel the thin veil of sweat from a day on her feet, still pressing into her uniform. She stood, legs frozen as she watched the door widen, pushing a strand of hair past her cheek and brushing a glaze of sweat along the edge of her temple.

2

"Sorry," she called, reflexively, "we're closed!" Her last word came out in a bit of a squawk as she watched the figure sidle into the studio.

A second later, she felt a flash of relief. It wasn't the bearded bear-gut after all. In fact, as she looked, she felt a sudden, impulsive sense of self-consciousness. The man now standing in front of her looked as if he'd stepped off a movie set. Impossibly handsome, with a thin, neatly trimmed beard and eyes like sapphires speckled with starlight. He didn't have a single hair out of place, and though she was used to the many fragrant odors of her workplace, she detected one she hadn't smelled before—a faint hint of a citrus aftershave. He smiled at her and nodded politely as he stepped into the studio and gave a small wave with a gentle hand.

Amelia often could determine the career of someone based purely on their hands. Something a sommelier often paid attention to in their clients—the bruises, the thickness of calluses, the softness of fingertips. She had spotted musicians, laborers, and once even a banker based purely on the hands.

This man had the hands of a painter, or, perhaps, a surgeon. Careful, lean fingers. He also held a small black bag—like that of a physician, or like the veterinarian who had once visited her mother when their cat had been sick.

She smiled politely at the man, but inwardly was in turmoil. She smoothed the front of her uniform and hastily tried to adjust her hair, but then felt a pulse of embarrassment as she realized she'd likely sweated through her uniform and was showing him the unsightly splotches by lifting her arms. Just as quickly she dropped her elbows and stood straight-backed, returning his smile.

"I'm—I'm sorry," she stammered. "We're closed."

The man's countenance dropped. It was like watching the sun set, a radiance disappearing behind a horizon of disappointment.

"But we only just closed," she said, quickly, as if trying to catch his disappointment before it hit the ground. "I suppose I could pour you a glass of our special. In fact," she added, with no small amount of pride, "I had a say in the recipe."

The man's face brightened again. He nodded at her, dipping his head in a sort of little bow. He spoke then, in an American accent, his French clipped and clean, but also hesitant as he fished for the proper words. "That would be a pleasure," he said. He smiled at her, and then

3

he moved over to one of the tables she had recently cleared.

Amelia watched as he moved, tracking his form through the neat suit and dress pants. It almost looked like he'd recently come from a wedding or funeral. She made a mental note to ask if the opportunity arose.

Amelia glanced back at the door. She knew it was against the studio's policy to have people in after hours. Unlocking the cash register off-timer would be a headache as well. Then again, though she hated to admit it, over the last year, she'd had a number of customers like Mr. Bearded Beer-Gut. She was starting to get tired of unwanted attention. Was it really so bad to use her job, for the first time, to entertain some attention she actually looked forward to?

She looked at him, smiling slightly. He really was quite handsome. Perhaps not as tall as she would've liked, but those eyes, that jawline, the posture, the confident swagger, all of it cumulatively made up for any small defect she might have spotted.

Another drawback of being someone whose job it was to critique: some thought she was overly critical in the partners she chose, but Amelia could pick out a ten-euro bottle of wine in comparison to a hundred-euro bottle. She could detect the taste in an instant, and in the same way, she wanted quality in the men in her life.

The handsome man sat at the table and leaned back, placing his small, black physician's bag on the table. It was then she noticed he was wearing gloves. Riding gloves? Or perhaps driving gloves?

The gloves were black, with stitched seams, and he tapped his fingers against the table for a moment. Slowly, she watched as he peeled off the gloves and placed them into the physician's bag. He zipped the bag back up, though not fully. This time, she glimpsed something glinting within. A matchbook?

He wasn't a smoker, was he? She hated it when that happened. Not the vice itself—the prettiest ones always had some hidden crutch. She simply preferred finding out about it after she got what she wanted.

Amelia allowed her eyes to stretch up and down the American once more, taking him in, wondering what he looked like without that suit on. Then, smirking to herself, she moved over behind the counter, withdrawing one of the special stock from the wooden slot at the back of the display case. Then, retrieving two clean glasses, she moved back toward where he waited.

He noticed the second glass. "Will you be joining me?" he called

4

across the room, still cranking his smile to a ten.

She shrugged back at him over the counter. "If you don't mind. My shift is almost over as it is."

The man chuckled. "It will be our little secret."

She brushed a strand of hair back into submission behind her ear and then returned to the table, her heels clicking against the floor as she strode back toward the man. She placed the tray and the two glasses on the table next to him. She hesitated, then realized she'd left her wine opener back with the other dirtied glasses.

"*Merde*," she cursed. "Sorry, one second."

She turned and hurried away, but a few seconds later, behind her, she heard a quiet pop. She glanced back, stunned, but realized the cork was now off, and the man was wafting his hand over the top of the bottle, inhaling deeply and then smiling.

"Spatburgunder, no?" he called out, smiling.

As she rejoined him a second time, leaving the bottle opener with the dishes, she slowly sat at the table and raised her eyebrows, impressed. "You know your grapes," she said. "Are you a sommelier too?"

He shook his head primly. His hands were clasped around the glass he poured, and she noted how he kept twisting it, studying the liquid within. One of his eyebrows arched delicately on his forehead.

"You know, there are stories about wine... Have you heard of Dionysus, the Greek god?"

She wrinkled her nose, shaking her head as she settled in the chair opposite him.

He smiled. "Just a myth, of course. But some think Dionysus's infatuation with wine was due to its god-making potential. The fruit in the garden of Eden, some say, was closer to a type of grape. It certainly wasn't an apple."

She smiled, puzzled for a moment.

Seemingly sensing her confusion, he gave a dismissive little laugh. "Wine is what you went to school for?" he asked.

She puffed her chest a bit and said, "Actually no—agricultural engineering." She still wished she hadn't sweated so much, but it was nice to talk about herself. Not everyone shared her interest in wine. She studied his lips, his jawline, her eyes tracing up to his soul-searching gaze. For a second, she glanced back at the physician's bag with the slightly open zipper. She still couldn't quite see what was inside and

5

realized perhaps it wasn't polite to stare, so she looked back at him. "You haven't told me your name," she said.

He curved one side of his lips up into an alley cat grin. "You can call me Gabriel."

"It's a pleasure to meet you, Gabriel," she said.

"The pleasure is all mine, Amelia."

She smiled, but the expression became rather fixed. A slow, chilly wind seemed to suddenly creep through the studio. How had he known her name? Her name badge only had her last name. An intentional effort by the staff, after some unwanted phone calls from various customers.

"Excuse me?" she said.

He smiled at her again, his startling blue eyes shifting in the fading sunlight, almost changing hue to a deep purple. "And besides wines, what other things do you enjoy?"

She rubbed at one of her arms, unbuttoning the sleeve, deciding this only made her more uncomfortable, before buttoning it again. "Music, art, poetry."

"Wonderful. All of it, wonderful. You're young, aren't you?"

She wrinkled her nose. "I doubt I'm much younger than you."

He shrugged modestly. "What are you, twenty-five? Twenty-six?"

She felt another bout of discomfort. Why was he asking her these questions? So quick, moving seamlessly from discussing wine to digging into her personal life. It wasn't a huge bother from someone who looked like Gabriel, but Amelia wasn't stupid, either. She suddenly realized she was alone with a stranger and glanced toward the gray sedan parked behind the dumpsters. She couldn't quite make out the license plate.

She watched as the man's fingers twisted around and around the wine glass. He still had some wine left in his glass, along with a small bead of red on his upper lip, which, after a moment, he licked away and gave a satisfied sigh.

"Well, I hope you enjoyed it," she said, softly. While his was nearly empty, her own glass was nearly untouched. "I really do need to be closing, though. It's policy."

"Dear Amelia," said Gabriel, "I fully understand. It is important to stick to one's policies. I must ask you one other thing. Have you ever thought about the afterlife? Have you at least considered it?"

Her stomach dropped, and now for the first time, she allowed the emotion to cross her face in a creased frown.

He acknowledged her expression, curious, and smiled in return. "You really are quite pretty when you frown, you know that? Well, have you considered the afterlife?"

"I'm sorry, what do you mean? That's a very strange question."

She shivered, beginning to push back from the table. Perhaps it was simply an American thing. She often heard they would ask very personal questions, even of strangers. The French didn't particularly like that sort of intrusion. Emotions and the like were all well and good, but certainly not among complete strangers, not even gorgeous ones. Then again, he had said she was pretty. But such words were beginning to lose their spell, and she was now past uncomfortable.

"I have, Amelia, see?" he said, softly. "The great painter Albrecht Durer completed the piece about the key and the pit, you know. In it, he depicted the only way to the beyond. Have you read Revelation? Or have you considered the Norse end? So many theories, so many thoughts. The best ones, though, if you ask me," he said, prattling on as if she were still interested and not scared, "they're the ones, in my humble estimation, that speak of an eternal life. A continuation of this thing. Infinite health. No more sickness or sadness. Can you imagine?"

She crossed her arms now. Of course, the one good-looking man who ever paid her attention was just trying to peddle his faith. She didn't say it out loud, but she thought it. Who came into a wine studio after hours, with a young woman, and began speaking to them about the afterlife?

She pushed away from the table, shaking her head. "I'm sorry," she said, softly, "I'm not interested. Whatever church you're a part of, sorry. I really do need you to leave now."

The man looked up at her, and his eyes were still twinkling with mirth. If anything in her countenance threw him off, he didn't show it. He dipped his head in quiet acquiescence. Then he reached into his physician's bag and withdrew his two black gloves. He pulled them on delicately, like a jockey before a horse race. Once they were on his hands, he retrieved the glass he had been drinking from, his fingers pressed against it, and then he tossed the contents of the wine off to the side.

She nearly shouted, watching the splatter against the grain wood of the floor.

"You shouldn't have done that," she snapped, angry now. It didn't

7

matter how good-looking someone was, there was no sense in wasting wine, nor in staining the floor.

He didn't reply right away, but instead placed the glass in his small bag.

"Hang on," she protested, "you can't take that."

"Oh," he said, "how about if I just buy it from you?" He tried to zip the bag, but it didn't fully close over the stem of the glass. Now, the physician's bag was open, wider, and she stared in at the contents. Her heart nearly escaped her chest. A cold, freezing sensation spread over her spine and up toward the base of her skull.

There was rope, and duct tape, and an assortment of small knives seemingly bound together by a thin strap. She spotted other instruments she had no name for, some with small hooks and others with probing needles. She spotted an IV bag and rubber hosing.

She felt a flicker of fear, and then it came flooding into her chest all at once, dropping to her stomach like the sudden hot swish of whiskey, spinning toward her belly. She quickly looked away, hoping the man hadn't spotted her attention.

She dipped her head in what she hoped would be perceived as a polite nod, rather than a terrified adjustment.

"Apologies," she said. "I must powder my nose."

The man just looked at her and gestured gallantly toward the back. "Do what you must," he said. "I'll be leaving soon as it is. I don't want to intrude."

Trying to hide her trembling hands, she began to move away quickly.

Fingerprints, she thought to herself. Such a strange thought. An odd thought, but one that struck her as true. He didn't want to leave the glass behind, because it had his fingerprints on it. This thought only further propelled her into another bout of terror.

She needed to get out. But where could she go? Her car was parked in the same lot as his gray sedan. She would have to exit the back, circle the building, and he would see her through the glass. She would have to cross in front of the dumpsters to reach her car. He might be fast enough to reach her before she could. Especially with her twinged back. She would barely make it.

She needed help. Was Andre here? No, she hadn't seen his car. She needed to call the police.

She walked stiffly, straight-backed, no longer caring about the sweat blotches against her uniform. She moved hastily toward one of the side rooms in the back of the wine-tasting studio. The room here was cold, where they would often chill some of the older vintages before serving them to richer clients. She pushed under the stray, dangling plastic barrier of rectangular strips, like the spinning rags at a car wash. She pushed at the cold plastic and stepped deeper into the cooling room.

With scrambling fingers, she groped for her pocket, hastily pulling out her phone. It took her a couple of tries to remember her own passcode, as fearful as she was. Adrenaline was coursing through her, pulsing up and down her body.

"Come on," she muttered darkly. "Come on."

Then she heard a quiet click. A tap on the side of her neck. A patient, even tap from a gloved finger, the sensation of smooth leather.

A blossom of absolute horror pulsed through her.

She whirled around, and was struck in the side of the head, hard, with an open hand. A second blow followed, but not a wild, untrained punch. A strange shooting motion, straight into her throat.

She gurgled, gasping, and heard a quiet, soothing voice, as more pressure was applied to her neck. "It will all be over soon, dear Amelia. Don't struggle, it might break your windpipe. I wouldn't want that."

Then she blacked out.

***

Twisting pain, pulsing needles in her eyes, her head.

She felt weak, sluggish, and her headache only increased. It was like a headache she'd once gotten when her nose had been congested, and she had breathed through a thin blanket at night. Not enough oxygen.

Her eyes fluttered sluggishly, and her eyelids felt heavy, weighted with lead. The insides of her eyeballs were scratchy, and hurt, and she blinked against a sudden glare.

She tried to look around, and found that though her head could move, her body was restrained. This filled her with an even greater terror. But the fear also moved like a steady prickle up her body, through her like seeping molasses across a floor.

She tried to rise, but found that her back was pressed against something cool. A second later, she realized she wasn't wearing her

9

shirt. For some reason, this sent an even greater bolt of fear through her.

Glancing down, she realized her bra straps had been lowered past her shoulders, and there were metal clamps against her arms, holding them in place. Her legs couldn't move either; she tried to kick them. She glanced down, fearing the worst, but saw she was still wearing her pants; there was at least that.

Exposed like this, she looked around and realized she was in an unfamiliar room. Bright glows, like movie theater lights, were blazing down on her. She looked at her arm suddenly, and nearly screamed. A needle was gouged into her wrist, leading to an IV and a bag with rubber hosing.

For a moment, she wondered if they were pumping something into her body. But it became clear enough, after a moment of disoriented staring, that they were pumping something out.

Someone was taking her blood.

"Help," she croaked in a weakened voice. The words barely managed to escape her lips before dying from their own frailty.

How much blood had she already lost?

She tried to look one way and then the other, but the blinding light still pulsed ahead of her. The cool metal pressed against the back of her half naked torso. And then, a blurring shadow.

It took her a moment to adjust, but she realized the shadow was that of the man.

He was still as handsome as she remembered. Still, not a single hair out of place. Still wearing the same black gloves: riding gloves? Driving gloves?

He was whistling softly to himself, tapping against a needle. He flicked the tip of the needle a couple of times, and she realized it was at the end of an injection. He held the shot up, examining it against the light, and then moved toward her.

A second later, though, he paused. "Ah, dear Amelia, you're awake. A pity. I had hoped you might stay out a bit longer. This isn't a pleasant process. I didn't want to put you out."

She groaned, trying to speak. "Fuck you," she managed to say.

He tutted quietly, still speaking in that American accent. It had been so charming at first, but now it felt like he was taunting her. "Amelia," he said, quietly, "look, I don't mean to cause you discomfort or displeasure. I promise you," he said, crossing a finger over his chest,

10

"I did not manhandle you inappropriately in any way."

He patted her on the cheek and made a modest gesture toward her unclothed torso. "Just looking for the best vein. It's an art form, truly. The way you speak of wine, I understand." He smiled at her. "I didn't do anything untoward. I hope you believe me."

She didn't nod, she didn't respond. She strained against the bindings on her wrists and legs. But she was held fast.

He placed one of his gloved fingers to his perfect lips, and his blue eyes peered out at her. "Dear Amelia, I had asked if you'd considered the afterlife. It didn't seem to interest you. I suppose that might be a good thing. If you think of it, on the other side, I hope you would tell me about it. Anyway, it's been a pleasure getting to know you. I hope to see you again. Thank you." He added this last part quickly and dipped his head. "Thank you dearly."

And then, with the same fast motion he'd used to knock her unconscious, a hand darted to his waist, pulled out something sharp. There was a flash of metal, and a sudden pain across her throat.

She gagged, choked, and then died.

CHAPTER TWO

Adele gagged, choked, and reached up, waving a hand in front of her face as the cloud of dust kicked up by the truck wafted over her. She frowned, lowered her head, and kept running. She could feel her breath squeezing from her lips, emitted in quiet puffs that met the chill morning air. One foot in front of the other, a jogging stride.

Inhale, exhale, reach up, wipe sweat. Inhale, exhale. She continued to jog, picking up the pace, her eyes fixed ahead.

Five-thirty in the morning. That's when the plant opened. She'd already memorized the factory schedule. She'd already read the names of the various workers on shift. She'd already stretched the limit of her discretion as a DGSI agent. Technically not actually employed by the agency, but in a freelance capacity now that she had moved back to Paris.

She jogged up the road, continuing a familiar path she had carved out over the last two weeks.

As she ran, she glanced toward the facility beyond.

The path she had chosen, circling the enormous plant in the distance, was little more than a two-hour run. She did it every morning. Easy. Momentum bred discipline. Discipline bred endurance. Small effects compounded over time.

And yet, today she had decided was the day she entered the plant. The case of her mother's murder needed planning, but not dawdling. She'd done her homework; now was time to act. No more scouting, no more tracking the trucks and watching the loading docks. Now, she went into the belly of the beast.

Candy bars. A strange thing to consider packaged in something so gray and gloomy, behind a thin wire fence topped with barbed wire.

The sun was also rising, seemingly reluctant to confront the morning, as if it had hit a snooze button in the clouds. And yet, Adele was itching to go.

Today was the day. It didn't matter she was wearing jogging clothes. It didn't matter she was sweating. Today she would speak to the manager, find the truck driver in question. Today she would find out

12

the truth. She jogged along the trail, refusing to get off the road even as a truck barreled down.

There was enough space for the two of them. The truck leaned on its horn, and she ignored it; eventually, the truck moved a bit to the side, passing her. She swallowed a mouthful of dust and spat off to the side, waving a hand in front of her eyes, blinking tears against the sudden swirl.

She turned up the road and moved toward the fence. The gate was running on a trolley, closing automatically. The guard sitting behind the desk, inside his small cubicle in the gatehouse, looked at her, a slight flicker of surprise in his expression.

She gave a little wave, hoping to put him at ease, but he didn't return the gesture. He reached down, grabbed a steaming mug, and took a long sip of the contents. She could practically feel the disgruntlement emanating from him. Clearly, this was not a morning person, but Adele was on a mission.

"*Bonjour*," she said, with a dip of her head. "Good morning."

"How can I help you?" the guard said, skipping pleasantries.

Adele swallowed and spat, realizing there was still dust tinging her lips. Sweaty, spitting, in running shoes and a running outfit, she supposed it didn't present her in the most professional light.

"Apologies," she said, curtly. "My name is Agent Sharp. I work with DGSI and Interpol." She reached into her side plastic pouch which was strapped around her leg with Velcro. The same place where she held her phone to listen to music. Of course, Adele didn't particularly enjoy music when she was running. She considered the distraction cheating. Endurance was built through pain; distraction numbed the effect.

"I need to enter and speak with the manager."

She flashed her credentials and held them up for the guard to see. He looked at them, and then his eyes flicked to her. His gaze scanned her outfit, and then glanced back at the credentials. He scratched at the side of his chin and muttered something beneath his breath.

"Interpol?" he said. "Are you from France?"

She thought it a strange question, and instead of answering, said, "Open the gate, please."

He held up a finger and said, "Hang on, I have to ask."

He turned promptly away from her, picked up a dial phone next to his computer screen, and lifted the dusty black device. He pressed it to his cheek, and, muttering to himself after taking another long sip of coffee, he dialed a number.

She waited patiently, sweaty, breathing heavily, feeling the itch of dust which stuck to slick skin. Then, after a brief conversation, the gate guard lowered the phone. "First building, first office."

***

Adele clicked her fingers together, tapping one hand impatiently against her upper thigh. She could feel the sweat slick against her brow, could feel one of the factory workers ogling her tight running outfit from behind. Her blonde hair was tucked in the white headband. She ignored the attention of the employee, staring at the sealed wooden door with the single black laminate plate which read *Coordinateur de l'Assemblée Gregor Fontaine*.

Adele rolled her shoulders and shot a look off to the side at the loading dock doors. She spotted another truck piled with brown boxes, pulling away. She thought of the cloud of dust, choking on the dirt. She thought of the many other trucks she had spotted, lining the loading zone behind the factory.

A lot of trucks, a lot of candy bars. A needle in a haystack. And yet, she could feel she was getting closer.

At last, the wooden door swung open, and a small, stiff-backed man with an ankle boot hobbled out. He had an aluminum crutch under one arm, and moved toward her.

For a moment, some of her impatience vanished to be replaced by a modicum of sympathy. "You okay?" she asked, jerking her head toward the boot.

The manager looked at her, but didn't reply. Instead, he leaned against his crutch, adjusting the boot and sliding it with a scraping sound against the cold stone factory floor. "How can I help you?" he said. "Gate said DGSI."

Adele nodded. "I'm looking into a case."

Before she could continue, the manager held up a hand that wasn't gripping the crutch. He made a wiggling motion with his fingers. "Credentials, please, if you don't mind."

Adele sighed, but fished out her credentials from the plastic compartment against her thigh. She flashed them toward the manager, and he took his sweet time about it, but at last, he finished reading, wagged his head, and she returned them to the pouch.

He looked her up and down, not in a lecherous way, but certainly an intrusive one. She shifted uncomfortably, waiting. "You're on the job?" he asked, wrinkling his nose at her outfit.

"In a way," she said, briskly. "I'm looking into one of your delivery trucks."

He shifted his weight again, groaning as he did. He shot her a resentful look, as if somehow the sprain in his ankle was her fault.

"We can go sit in your office if you like," she said.

He quickly shook his head. He glanced back at the door, which was shut, and then looked at her again. "No, here's fine. What do you want to know about one of my trucks?"

"Specifically, trucks that deliver to Paris."

"Paris is a big city," he replied.

"Yes, but I'm tracking packages that go to a specific shop. I followed the truck that arrived and dropped off a few weeks ago."

"It is a large store? Trucks go to a lot of stores in Paris."

She nodded. "I know, but no, it's not a large store. Called Gobert's."

The man didn't blink; he didn't react in any way. He had the dead-eyed look of someone clueless.

Adele frowned. "Look, I just want to know the names of the drivers that deliver to Gobert's."

"A few weeks ago, you say?" he said.

She hesitated, and tapped her thumb against her chin. "Actually, it's from ten years ago."

Now he was staring at her as if she'd gone insane. "Ten years? Dear, I don't think you know how this place operates. It isn't exactly anyone's dream job. We have high turnover—nearly seventy percent." He waved a small hand toward the assembly line through a side glass partition between the entry room and the main floor of the factory. A few people were scattered among conveyor belts, testing products or marking clipboards. Another few operated large machines, and then a few more loaded packaged boxes onto a forklift.

"All right, well, how many employees do you have?" she said, testily. "It would've been around ten years ago. Someone involved with delivering the packages."

The manager frowned. "Who did you say you were with?"

Adele fixed him with a look, but didn't reach for her credentials

15

again, allowing the weight of her glower to tip the scales. And then he blinked and looked away; he muttered to himself, but waved a hand and moved back toward his office.

Adele tried to follow, but he slammed the door shut before she could step through. She stood with her nose nearly pressed against the door. With a reluctant sigh, sweaty, and tired from her run, she returned back to the center of the waiting room.

She stared at the wooden door and the plaque with the name on it, counting in her head, for no other reason than to distract herself. She counted the chocolate bars moving across the conveyor belts, and counted the employees within, through the glass partition.

At last, the door creaked open, and the manager hobbled out again, swinging his bad leg in the boot and pushing off his crutch.

"A few names," he said. "Most don't work here anymore—like I said, high turnover. But two of them still do. One of them is an old fellow. Used to run trucks, but was too weak to lift the boxes. Had to move him over to the conveyor belt—handed in his two-week notice a month ago. He's not in today."

Adele hesitated. "Who's the other?"

The manager sighed, then checked down at the phone he had open in his hand. He glanced at the note on it, then looked up at her. "As luck would have it, he's actually in. A younger guy. Name of Andrew Maldonado."

"And where is Mr. Maldonado?"

The manager waved at the glass partition, pointing toward a dark-haired fellow leaning over a conveyor belt. He wore protective eyeglasses and carried a clipboard tucked under one arm where he stood next to one of the larger machines.

"He gets off shift in about three hours. If you don't mind waiting, you're not allowed on the floor, as it could be dangerous for—"

Completely ignoring him, Adele stepped past the injured manager and pushed toward the glass partition. There was a security key card reader in front of her, and she gestured, snapping her fingers at the manager. "Open—open this."

The manager was staring at her, shaking his head. "I'm sorry, but unless you have a warrant, you're not allowed on the floor during operating hours, unless you're licensed by—"

"I don't care about your safety licensing. Open the door or I'll shoot it."

16

The words surprised her even as she said them, but the manager's eyes bugged. He gave her a nervous look and then, glancing up and down to see if she even had a weapon, he hobbled over. He slid a key card in the slot and opened the door.

"At least wear safety glasses," he said, wincing. "You can never be too careful in a place like—"

But whatever he'd been about to say, she ignored, moving through the door and stepping hurriedly toward the indicated fellow by the conveyor belts. She called out as she approached, "Andrew Maldonado!"

The man didn't seem to hear her over the whir and grind of the machines. Adele huffed in frustration, stepping purposefully across the factory floor, her eyes fixed on her target.

The only person in this entire company, besides a geriatric, who had driven trucks ten years ago. The only person still connected to the Carambars, to Gobert's, to her mother.

Anything else was a dead end. She couldn't let this one get away. She stomped toward Andrew, who still hadn't heard her, and gripped his shoulder, spinning him. She found herself looking into an extremely pale face above a patchy beard. Mr. Maldonado had stretchy skin beneath his eyes as if perhaps he had lost a significant amount of weight very quickly.

Andrew looked at her and lowered his clipboard, surprised. He took in her appearance and then glanced through the glass partition at his manager. "He can't help you now," she snapped. "I need you to tell me what you were doing ten years ago when you were delivering Carambars to Gobert's."

The man just looked at her, adjusted his safety glasses, and then, stuttering, "Wh-what?"

She repeated the question, but more forcefully.

"Ten years ago? I don't know what you're talking about."

She pointed a finger at him, practically jamming it up his nostril. "Why did you stop driving trucks? Why are you here?"

He hesitated and then muttered, "I don't like driving. Makes me uneasy. *Who* are you?"

"I work with Interpol," she snapped. "What were you doing ten years ago? Did you know Elise Romei? Did you know the shop Gobert's? Did you tamper with the chocolate bars?"

He looked over her shoulder again, staring stunned toward the manager, who was shrugging helplessly in the doorway. Adele again tried to ignore him, placing herself between Andrew and his manager.

"Who are you?" he repeated. "You're with EMA, aren't you? Is this a trial run?"

Adele was beginning to lose her already malnourished patience. She knew she shouldn't. She knew she was behaving erratically. But it didn't matter. Why was he acting so stupid? "Answer my question!" she demanded.

He just continued to look at her with that helpless expression. For a moment, she was reminded of Angus, her old boyfriend. This only irritated her more.

She jammed a finger into his chest, and he took a couple of skipping steps back. One of his hands shot out, trying to brace himself against the conveyor belt. But it was still moving, and he fell, stumbling, jolted forward by the motion. A couple of the chocolate bars were knocked free, and scattered onto the ground.

"Careful!" the manager called. "That's not protocol!"

"Why are you lying to me?" Adele shouted at Andrew. Images flashed in her mind; bleeding, bleeding... fingers missing, a mutilated body of a once beautiful woman, dumped on the side of the road. *Switching notes... Funny?*

"Stop playing dumb!" she shouted. "I know you were there! Why did you do it? If you don't answer me, I'm going to make your life a living hell!"

The bearded fellow looked at her, his eyes wide, like a doe caught in headlights. He was shaking his head, his voice trembling. Now, he held his gloved hand and waved the clipboard as if fanning himself. "I'm sorry," he said. "I don't know what I did. I can't remember ten years ago. I delivered to a lot of shops."

Adele could feel her rage simmering. But for a moment, she paused, then glanced around. She could feel eyes on her, staring. She looked one way, then the other, and swallow back a rising sense of fury in her chest. Many of the other assembly workers and conveyor belt operators were staring at her. The manager in the doorway had taken a couple of hobbling steps in, pointing at her, saying, "I'm calling your superiors!"

She sighed, deflating like a leaking balloon. She could feel the anger seeping from her; her frustration diminishing. "You don't remember anything?" she said, in a quieter, defeated tone.

18

He just looked at her and continued to shake his head, still seemingly stunned.

She passed a weary hand over her sweaty face. Perhaps running for two hours on an empty stomach hadn't been the smartest thing leading up to an interrogation. She could feel a headache that came from hunger and exhaustion. She still had an hour to run back to where her car waited, halfway between the factory and the city.

She muttered a quiet apology and dusted off Andrew's shoulder, and then turned, striding quickly back out of the factory, past the manager, through the glass partition, and down the loading dock where she had entered.

She began to jog before she even reached the gate. Another hour of jogging. It wouldn't clear her mind, though. Her mind was swimming, swirling, protesting. Her mind was on fire, and anger pulsed through her. An anger directed at nothing. At no one. A nameless, faceless void, taunting her from the shadows.

Adele's hands curled into fists, and she broke into a sprint, hastening toward the gate. As she approached, she was grateful to see the guard had hit the button. The metal slid open as it had for the trucks. And though the same amount of dust wasn't kicked up behind her, she felt she was faster than the vehicles had been. She exited the factory and moved back up the long road, one step, two steps, faster, faster.

CHAPTER THREE

Adele felt a flicker of annoyance as she pushed open this new gate. A much nicer, more ornate gate than the factory's. The annoyance was directed toward the events from the morning, not toward what lay beyond. In front of her, one of the few oases in Paris awaited her. One of the few places she could relax. She approached Robert's mansion, closing the gate behind her and hearing the electronic click, as the security lock reset from the code she'd entered. Robert always supplied her with the code, texting it to her. The most recent one had changed a week before.

Robert was very safety conscious, and normally, he changed it every few days. So it was a bit of a surprise a week had passed without another alteration.

Adele took the steps up to the mansion, rolling her shoulders as she did. At least now she wore more comfortable clothing. She had changed in her car, and though she could still smell sweat, and her hair was still grainy from the dust against her forehead, she felt a bit better to be out of her running clothes. She still hadn't eaten anything, and hoped Robert would have the chocolate cereal he often kept for her.

She reached the front door, staring up at the black, reinforced glass; the doors were tall, stretching high above her. She steadied herself, standing on the marble steps, and then tapped her fingers against the deep wood, listening to the dull *thunk*.

The door swung open instantly, as if he'd been waiting for her just inside.

"My dear," Robert said in delight. "Come in, darling." He gestured at her, gallantly sweeping her toward the long hall and then giving her a slight bow.

She smiled as she looked at her old mentor, feeling a faint flicker of gratitude. "How are you doing?" she said, quietly.

When he looked up from his bow, some of her smile faded. His cheeks were gaunt, and his eyes were sunken. Not too much, but enough she noticed. His hair was immaculate, as always, and his mustache was curled and oiled. But his skin was a bit paler than she

20

remembered, and he looked even thinner. She could see the very edge of his collar bone pressing against the skin beneath the loose collar of his poorly fitting shirt.

"Robert, are you okay?"

He kept smiling at her, but even the smile now seemed rather fixed. A second later, he began to cough, pressing a hand up against his mouth, and then gesturing with another for her to join him in the study.

"Robert, what's wrong?"

"I'm fine, my dear—you're the one who called. Come to the study. I started a fire and set aside a bowl of cereal. Why you eat that sugary nonsense, I'll never know. But it's yours."

Adele felt a flicker of gratitude, but it was replaced just as quickly by worry. She moved after her old mentor, following Robert's form down the hall and into the study. He clicked a button on the wall, and the front door closed behind them.

Adele heard the door click, and glimpsed a sliver of light cutting out as they were sealed in the mansion together.

Two leather chairs faced the fire, and Robert settled in the chair on the left, a pile of books on the little table next to his hand.

"Robert, what's wrong?"

He began to answer, but broke into another fit of coughing. He held up a finger, as if to say, *one moment.*

Adele frowned, sitting in her own chair. She waited as Robert gathered himself. As she did, she could feel a flash of a hunger headache, and her stomach rumbled. Despite herself, and feeling a bit guilty, she reached for the chocolate cereal that he'd left for her on the table. A glass of milk sat next to it. She poured the milk into the bowl and gratefully began munching away.

After a few bites, and after Robert seemed to have recovered, she said, "You don't look well."

He snorted. "Adele, I'm fine. What did you want to talk about? You seemed upset on the phone."

She paused a moment and thought of how she had behaved back at the factory. She thought about the frustration she'd felt, and the anger directed toward the helpless employee. She thought about her mother, about Gobert's shop. She thought about the Carambars.

She passed a hand wearily across her countenance, trying to steady her own nerves. "If I'm honest, it wasn't pretty," she said, softly.

"I'm sorry, dear. Is it a case?"

She looked at him, and again spotted just how gaunt his face seemed. His cheekbones were too sharp, his eyes too dark. "Robert… you don't look well. Stop telling me—"

Before she could finish, her phone began to ring, the vibrating emanating from her sweater pocket. Frowning, she fished her phone out.

"Sorry," she muttered, "it's work." She clicked the phone, held it up to her ear. "Can it wait?" she asked.

"Afraid not," said the voice on the other end. She immediately recognized it as the voice of Executive Foucault's assistant. "He wants you in. You're needed over at the office."

Adele massaged the bridge of her nose with her free hand, the cold phone still pressed against her cheek. She wanted to shout in frustration, but instead said quietly, "I'm on my way."

She lowered the phone and looked at Robert.

"You're going in?"

She nodded.

"Anything to do with what happened this morning?"

She sighed and shrugged. "Not sure. This isn't over," she added, pointing at him. "If you need anything…" Her voice softened and she watched her old mentor. "I hope you know all you have to do is ask."

Robert Henry made a crossing motion over his chest, and then kissed his fingers. "I'm fine, darling. Would these lips lie to you, my dear?" He smiled, and for a moment, she saw her usual, jovial mentor sitting across from her in his leather seat. He still had two missing teeth, glimpsed above his smile. She had heard at least ten stories regarding how he had lost those teeth.

Sighing, she pushed up, taking another few mouthfuls of cereal. Her growling stomach would have to wait.

"Look," she said, "I'll be back. Thanks for the cereal."

"No worries," he said. "I hope everything turns out okay." Then he broke into another series of coughing.

The sound haunted her, and for a moment she paused in the doorway. She wanted to stop, to refuse the call into the office. To figure out what was up with her friend. But when Robert wanted to be quiet, he could keep his secrets with the best of them. She'd heard stories of him once being captured by a gang of drug runners in Bordeaux. The stories said he'd been tortured, but hadn't said a word. Stories about Robert often circulated around the DGSI. He had been one of their best

22

operators from the very start, and had led a long, tenured career before the agency had even formed.

"I'll be thinking of you," she said.

He gave a little wave of his fingers, then leaned back as if exhausted in his chair.

She felt a surge of fear rising up in her. Perhaps she needed to go for another run in the afternoon. But somehow, even the runs weren't doing what they used to. The fear seemed hard to suppress. She had to convince herself Robert would be okay. He had to be. She moved out of the mansion door, down the steps, toward the sealed gate. Hopefully, whatever awaited her at the office wouldn't have anything to do with the factory. She picked up the pace, hurrying out the gate and toward her parked vehicle.

CHAPTER FOUR

Adele pulled her sedan into the parking spot nearest the security checkpoint. She glanced up and noted Agent Renee's new lease—a five-year-old Corvette—sitting askew across one of the handicapped spots. She rolled her eyes at the poor parking job and the new sports car, but then suppressed a small smile which also inserted itself across her countenance as she exited her own car, shut and locked the door, and strode with quick steps toward the doors to the office.

Her hair still felt grainy against her forehead, and she was still in a sweatshirt and slacks. She hadn't had time to shower yet, but supposed Foucault would have to deal with her appearance given the abrupt nature of his summons.

She passed Agent Renee's Corvette and then moved through the sliding doors that led to the metal detectors and the four security guards waiting just within the lobby. She nodded to each in turn, flashed her credentials, and then moved into the DGSI building. The air still smelled faintly of fresh paint—the building itself was new, having only been established this side of the twenty-first century. She noted red painting strips with the texture of confetti lining the walls above the entry.

"They almost done?" she asked one of the guards.

The woman sighed and shrugged. She waved distractedly toward a ladder leaning against the back wall. "Supposed to be this week. Hopefully we can wait another decade before another touch-up."

Adele winced sympathetically, smiled, and then moved past security toward the elevator. She stepped right past the metal compartment and took the stairs instead.

One flight, two, three. She spiraled up the stairs, moving toward the top floor.

Down another hall, at the end of a carpeted floor, she reached the familiar opaque glass door. Adele smoothed her sweater, inhaled, and sniffed faintly at the air. Then she fanned out her sweater a bit, tugging at the front and lifting her arms to shake the article of clothing.

This done, she knocked politely against the opaque door.

"Ah!" came an immediate call. "I believe she may in fact be gracing us with her presence after all. Can't see you on that side of the door, Agent Sharp!"

Adele winced at the tenor to Foucault's voice. He was trying to be clever. Whenever he tried to be clever it meant he was in a bad mood. She hid her expression as she pushed open the door and stepped into the Executive's office.

The air was filled with smoke. Executive Foucault had a cigarette between two fingers and was breathing a puff toward the open window behind his desk. Some of the smoke was ushered out of the room by a small, spinning desk fan. A series of crushed orange cigarette butts suggested this wasn't Foucault's first morning indiscretion.

Agent Renee was sitting in the room as well. The tall, handsome French agent leaned against his chair across from Foucault's desk. His long legs were extended and his shoes pressed firmly against the varnished oak, just below the lip of the desk and out of sight so Foucault couldn't see the stains being left on the furniture.

Adele hesitantly approached, glancing at John, then Foucault.

"Sorry," she said, instinctively. "Was on a run."

"Looks like it." John nodded, giving her a sidelong look by tilting his head and peering at her over the back of his chair.

Adele smiled politely at Foucault, but quiet, so only John could hear, she muttered, "Shut up."

He winked at her. "Good to see you too."

Foucault, who'd lowered his cigarette, was frowning, glancing between John and Adele. He narrowed his eyes shrewdly and half opened his mouth, but then seemed to think better of it. He frowned, thinking through his words carefully, then he took another puff and slowly, he ventured, "You two know the policy about office relationships—yes?"

Instantly, Adele felt her cheeks warm. Stammering, she quickly said, "Er—what? Yes. No. We're not—if you're thinking—no, there's nothing like—"

At the same time, John said, "We're filthy, filthy lovers, sir. You've caught us dead to rights."

Adele wanted to kick his chair over, but Foucault looked at John and seemed to determine the tall Frenchman was being factitious. His eyes narrowed even more. "Agent Renee, you're not scuffing my desk, are you?"

John coughed and quickly dropped his extended legs, hastily pretending as if he'd just been stretching. "What?" he said. "Of course not." Then, as any true partner would, he threw Adele under the bus. "Sir, what was it you were telling me about a call from earlier? Some angry factory worker?"

Foucault's ire shifted, moving from John back to Adele. He pointed his cigarette at Adele, the curling smoke rising past his cheeks and casting a gray shadow over his already ominous expression. "That's right," he said. "I heard about your little excursion this morning. What do you think you were doing?"

Adele stammered, "Ex-excursion, sir?"

"What were you doing out there?" Foucault asked, his dark eyes narrowed beneath his hawklike brow. His overly bushy eyebrows seemed a tangle of dark hairs like the charred remains of the smoke curling past his face. "I checked; I'm not aware of any active cases involving that factory."

Inwardly, Adele desperately wanted to wipe the smirk off John's face, but out loud, she replied to her angered overseer, "It was nothing, sir. Just a small misunderstanding. I was following a lead in another case."

"What case?"

She winced, then quickly lied, "Something for Interpol. I'll have a file to you soon."

Executive Foucault rubbed at the stubble on his chin. He lowered his cigarette and pushed it into the ashtray, grinding it out amidst the others. He waved a hand in front of his face, as if sifting the smoke back toward the window.

"See that you do," he said. "The only way I can keep you as a correspondent is if I'm apprised of your actions. And," he added, sternly, "if you're going to invoke DGSI credentials, it has to be a DGSI case. Understand?"

Adele winced. She bobbed her head once.

Foucault sat down now, leaning back in his leather chair and staring across the desk. He looked at Agent Renee, and then crossed his own feet, placing them on top of the desk. It was very unusual for the normally professional Executive to take such a casual posture. It almost seemed like he was challenging John. Then he said, "We had a murder in Bordeaux."

Adele breathed a sigh of relief, and then felt a sudden flash of guilt at the reaction. "And you want us on the case?" she said, hesitantly, grateful he'd stopped yelling at her.

"It's not an isolated incident."

John perked up at this. "A second murder?" he asked.

Foucault steepled his fingers beneath his chin and nodded, his dark eyebrows rising slightly on his weathered forehead. "Yes. A second murder—a near match in Germany. Both of them within the last two weeks." He tilted his eyebrows significantly. "The killer is moving at a breakneck pace. He's fast. And it seems like his appetite is only increasing."

Adele crossed her arms over her sweater, trying to breathe shallowly in the smoke-infused room. "What do we have to go on?"

The Executive looked between the two of them. "Not much. You will be looking at the case with fresh eyes." He hesitated, then his eyes narrowed until they were little more than prisms of shadow beneath his angled brow. Delicately, he added, pointing from Adele to John, "Perhaps you two had best read up on the agency's policy for office romances, yes? I'm not accusing anyone of anything, of course," he added, hurriedly, adding a smile as sincere as a politician's oath. "But just in case... I find it to be pleasant reading—you might find some useful things in there... the sorts of things that can save careers... You never know."

Adele stammered, "John was joking. There is nothing."

John sighed. "That's downright hurtful, my love."

Again Foucault looked at John, as if trying to determine if he was joking—one often couldn't tell with Renee. And again, Adele resisted the urge to slap her partner.

"Whatever," Foucault said, waving a dismissive hand. "Get dressed, take a shower," he added, giving Adele a meaningful look. "Your flight leaves in two hours. And remember, you're on a clock. The killer is moving fast, and moving across borders—it's proving a nightmare to keep up with the agencies involved. Each week wasted is another loved one lost and another potential international incident—so no cutting corners on this one unless you have to." He tilted his bushy brow significantly in John's direction, then made a small shooing motion toward the door.

CHAPTER FIVE

Adele sat next to John in first class, both of them sharing the same computer screen on Adele's tray. The rising sense of urgency in Foucault's voice filled her with a bit of unease. A fast-moving killer crossing international borders would be a headache for the higher-ups to coordinate, true, but—more importantly—people were dying. John's eyes were narrowed as he scanned the document, frowning. Adele tried to scroll down, but he reached out and flicked her knuckles. "I'm not done, wait."

"You're illiterate," she muttered.

John snorted. "Some of us have better things to do with our lives than reading screens all day."

"John, I can do this in three languages."

"Yes? And I slept with three woman last week—which of us is the real illiterate?"

"I'm starting to suspect you don't even know what that word means."

John smirked. Then he lifted his hand from where he'd flicked her and gestured at the computer. "At your leisure, American Princess."

Adele rolled her eyes and scanned through the rest of the report. Sometimes it was hard for her to tell if John was flirting or just trying to annoy her. The tall, handsome agent had always looked like a James Bond villain. He had a burn mark that stretched down from the edge of his chin along his neck toward his muscled chest. His hair was often combed, and slicked with gel, with a few loose strands over his forehead.

"Victims don't seem the same at all," John said, some of the amusement fading from his tone. He tapped a finger to the screen. "Died the same way though."

Adele read the indicated portion of the report and nodded. "I don't see the connection," she said. "The first one is a German farmer. He's what, in his fifties? And then here, the French sommelier, mid-twenties. Different educational backgrounds, different languages, different countries. Different ethnicity. I don't get it."

John pointed a bit further down the screen. "Same MO, though. It's the same killer. Too much of a coincidence otherwise."

"I suppose." Adele trailed off, reading the details for the third time in the same quick flight. The airplane around them trembled a bit with turbulence, and Adele heard rattling trays and the quiet gasp that always accompanied first class in mild weather. She ignored it. She'd flown enough in her life to not get alarmed by a little bit of wind. "Needle marks. Both of them, on their left arms."

John nodded. "Throat slit, bled out. Seems obvious. He sedates them with injections, and then kills them."

Adele wrinkled her nose, scanning to the bottom of the document and flipping through the pictures from the victims—the least pleasant part of the job. But as she scanned, she slowly shook her head. "The needle was small. But why sedate them, if you're just going to cut their throats? There's no torture."

John winced. "Sexual assault?"

She shook her head. "None visible. Doesn't seem like that either."

"Would be strange if so. Such different victims. If the killer was using them for sadistic pleasure, he certainly doesn't have a type."

"That's a morbid thought. But... he's almost humane towards his victims." Adele shook her head, scanning the last few items of the report. Then, once finished, she slowly lowered her laptop lid and stared at the backrest in front of her. Again, John tried to flick her knuckles, but this time she was too quick, and she slammed the laptop on his fingers.

He yelped and jerked his hand back. "Serves you right," she muttered. "Especially after throwing me under the bus with Foucault."

John shrugged petulantly. "Not my fault you're off yelling at factory workers."

"It was nothing," she said, curtly.

She could now feel his gaze burrowing into the side of her cheek. But she refused to look at him. Not even John knew about her side investigation—she wasn't sure why she hadn't shared. Somehow, it simply felt too personal.

Adele exhaled slowly, reaching up to fiddle with the small air conditioning nozzle above her. She thought about the case again, mulling over the details. Why would the killer inject his victims, sedate them, just to slit their throats later? Why not just cut their throats to begin with? It didn't make much sense. If he wanted to play with his victims, then the sedation made sense. Adele had seen a similar MO on her first case back in France, but then the killer had tortured his victims. He had gotten off on it. This time, though, there was something almost clinical about the cuts. The least amount of pain possible. Almost, and the word barely applied, but it almost felt *humane*. As if the killer had wanted to sedate them so they didn't know they were going to be killed. This didn't fit with anything she knew about psychopaths.

"What are you thinking?" John asked.

She leaned back in the airplane chair, pressing her head against the cushioned headrest. She tried to close her eyes, to focus, and inhaled slowly. "Seems procedural," she said, softly. "Clinical. I don't think he's a sadist. I don't think he's getting off on it."

"Then why kill them?"

"A German farmer, a French sommelier," Adele said. "Why kill them indeed. I guess that's the question."

She listened to the buzz and hum of the airplane, another quiet rattle as they made their way out of turbulence, and the subsequent sigh of relief from a couple of wealthy travelers in the front section of first class. Adele tried to inhale fully, then exhale to calm herself. She never particularly liked cases that involve knives. Images flashed across her mind's eye at the thought. Cuts, scars, swirling, looping patterns painted in agony and flesh.

Adele winced, gritting her teeth, her eyes sightless as she stared at the back headrest in front of her. Normally, when she went for a jog in the mornings, it helped clear her head, and it helped her focus. Now, though, she could feel the anxiety swirling in her chest. She could picture the images, the screenshot memories of her mother's case, her mother's corpse. Memories perhaps best forgotten, or filed away deep, deep in her subconscious.

Still, despite her distraction, it was up to Adele to solve this particular case. Clinical or not, humane or otherwise, there was a killer on the loose, and it was her job to find him before he killed again.

CHAPTER SIX

Agent John Renee hated small cars. His long legs pushed up against the back seat in the squad car the Bordeaux Police Department had sent for them. Adele was in the front passenger seat, and he felt certain she had pushed her chair as far back as it would go on purpose.

He could feel his knees pressed up against the leather, and he glared at the back of Adele's head over the head rest. Her shoulder-length blonde hair was pulled back in a neat ponytail. She had showered before the flight, and he could smell the faint fragrance of strawberries and soap.

"Nice scenery," Adele said absentmindedly, gazing out the front window.

The local cop who had been sent to fetch them didn't reply, but just nodded once, his eyes fixed on the road ahead of them as they moved down the road. On either side, fields stretched across in the shadows of mountains; hilly terrain was replaced by flat, open expanses. John could see the effect of swirling wind meandering through various trees, and row after row of vines married to wooden supports on either side of the road.

Adele murmured, "It's been a while since I've been out here. It really is quite pretty." She pushed a finger against the window button and it slid a bit. A warm, fragrant breeze swirled through the vehicle, and Adele smiled to herself, the corner of her lips just visible to John.

"Yes, fine," John snapped, indifferent to his partner's existential moment. "Mind moving your chair forward a bit?"

She turned slightly and looked at him over her shoulder. Even her profile was quite pretty in an exotic sort of way. French, American, and German. Adele was the full package. John wrinkled his nose at the thought, though, and quickly distanced himself from it. He replaced the sentiment with another burst of frustration. "I'm serious, you're cutting off my circulation."

Adele's tone carried every level of condescension as she said, "Maybe if you weren't such a filthy, filthy lover, your blood flow would be better regulated."

31

Then she turned back and made absolutely no effort to adjust her seat.

John leaned back, jamming his knees into her chair, realizing exactly how childish this made him seem. As he looked at Adele, though, staring at her from the back of the squad car, he felt a flicker of unease. She had been acting strangely ever since the case in Germany with the missing children. He had been there, after she had fallen out with her father.

Part of him wondered if he ought to ask her about it. That's what a decent person would do, or so he assumed. He rarely spent much time around any of those.

The squad car pulled up a dusty dirt path, kicking up debris and rattling as it made its way along the unpaved road. John winced each time one of his knees jammed painfully into the back of Adele's seat. He gripped the handle above his window, and waited, until they pulled to a halt.

"This is it?" he asked, growling.

"Yes, sir," said the local. "It's where they found the body. The vineyard where she works is only two miles down the road."

Adele was already exiting the car, pushing open the door and stepping out. She closed the door behind her, giving John time to figure out how to squeeze out of the cramped backseat on his own.

At last, he managed to extricate himself, stepping out into the dusty, cool terrain beneath the sun veiled by a scattering of clouds. He blinked a couple of times, his eyes narrowed against the glare in the sky as he examined the crime scene.

"Is that a shipping container?" Adele asked, her eyes fixed on the red metal fixture in the middle of the dusty ground.

The local nodded, lifting yellow caution tape and allowing the two agents to pass under. Another two cops were standing by the container, notepads in hands, muttering quietly to each other.

John took in the scene. He glanced down the road toward the vineyard in the distance, and then along the side of the shipping container, toward a pile of discarded wooden crates

"Why is there a shipping container out here in the middle of nowhere?" Adele asked.

The local glanced at the agent and said, "Storage. For excess packaged products. Shipping containers are easy to cool quickly, and are relatively secure. Plus they're a tenth of the price of building an actual structure." He shrugged. "I know a few farmers in the area who use these things as temporary layovers."

Adele wrinkled her nose. "And this container, whose land is it on?"

The local shook his head. "Still trying to figure that out. Seems that it is within the boundary of the vineyard where the victim worked."

Adele stepped toward the open door of the shipping container. John followed.

The body had been removed at this point. But John had seen the crime scene photos on the flight, and he could block out the setting in his mind. He spotted dark splotches against the metallic ground. The back wall of the small enclosure still showed signs of blood spray.

"Find anything useful?" he asked, glancing back.

The local winced and shook his head. "Still going over it, but doesn't seem to be any fingerprints. The blood belongs to the victim. We'll have more tests, and maybe we'll get lucky." By the tone of his voice, it seemed like he wasn't counting on it.

John nodded and the local officer walked out of the shipping container, leaving the two agents to stand in the cool metal enclosure, scanning the small space.

Adele's eyes were half hooded, and she seemed to be staring off into the distance for a moment as she peered down the long container. John watched her speculatively and then quietly said, "Is everything okay?"

She jolted, as if he'd stunned her. "Excuse me?"

John raised his hands, as if defending himself against the accusation of actually caring. "Just wondering if you're doing okay. You look lost."

Adele snorted and turned away, taking a few steps along the metal container. Boots clanged against the floor. She came to a stop in front of the angry red spots on the ground, staring down.

"Not much here," she said.

John shook his head. "Doesn't seem like it."

"Any theories as to why he killed her?"

"No, you?"

Adele inhaled, her chest puffing, but then she breathed a deep sigh and shook her head. "The why only matters when it helps us catch them."

She then turned, scanning the ceiling of the metal container. She

33

paused for a moment, taking note of something. John followed her gaze. "Cobwebs," he said. "Means the thing hasn't really been used much."

Adele shrugged one shoulder. "Maybe, or maybe our killer just didn't care to clean it."

Again, John found himself studying the side of his partner's face. She seemed strained, stressed. "Have you been sleeping well?"

Now, she finally rounded fully on him, facing him and meeting his gaze directly. "I'm doing fine, John."

John shrugged. "You don't seem yourself is all. Are things okay with your dad? Have you managed to sort it out after—"

Adele cut him off curtly, her tone turning cold. "We're taking a bit of a break from each other," she said, making it clear she didn't want to speak on it anymore.

John, though, considered social boundaries more like suggestions. He trampled over the suggestions with his next question. "You're sure? You were really mad at him for a while. But he is your dad, and—"

She snorted again, rolling her eyes. "And what are you? Dr. Phil?"

John returned her look. "I have absolutely no clue who that is."

Adele rolled her eyes and turned, marching out of the container and gesturing that he should follow. "There's nothing here," she said. "Let's scan the surrounding area; maybe the killer got careless."

John followed after her. Clearly, his questions had irritated her. Then again, perhaps she was simply displeased at the thought of combing through dirt and old boxes in search of a clue they both knew wouldn't be there. The killer had proven one thing; he was methodical, careful. Yet, still, John supposed they had their due diligence. And if Adele was anything, it was diligent.

Together, Adele and John began circling around the shipping container, their feet scuffing in the dust, moving toward the stacks of crates. As they scanned the ground, Adele broke off a bit, moving in the opposite direction of her partner and circling the container the other way. "I'll meet you on the other side," she muttered. Her eyes were glued to the ground as she moved away from her partner, distancing herself, searching for clues in the dirt.

***

The search came up with nothing. No new clues. No new hunches.

34

The two-mile drive to the vineyard where the sommelier had been abducted passed in silence. This time, John had the good sense to sit in the passenger seat behind the driver's side. The local uniform pulled to a halt outside a couple of dumpsters, parking a few spaces away from the odoriferous trash cans.

Another cop was waiting for them at the door of the wine-tasting studio. John inhaled the air as he stepped out of the vehicle, and was confronted with equal parts day-old garbage, and the faint hint of a fruity scent on the air. Behind the main structure of the vineyard, he spotted the actual farm. Grapes and vines and rows of green and purple on wooden stands as far as the eye could see.

John whistled softly beneath his breath, and then moved toward the entrance to the studio by which the other police officer stood. The fellow unlocked the door and gestured for them to enter.

Adele and John moved into the wood and stone room beyond.

Above, crisscrossing oak beams and stone-veneer pillars provided a rustic feel to the vineyard. John and Adele moved toward a series of circular tables speckled with blue stone. An oak counter was to their right, and a pile of used glasses sat in a plastic tray on the counter.

Again, Adele distanced from him, immediately moving in the opposite direction of where he'd been heading.

John sighed to himself, but pushed back his irritation, circling around the nearest tables and scanning the chairs beneath the windows.

"Find anything here?" John asked the local.

But the cop just winced and shook his head. "Nothing came up yet. The owner of the vineyard should be in within the hour—he's having to fly from Italy."

John nodded to show he heard, then continued his trek, moving along the chairs and tables.

"Looks like everything was wiped down," he said, directing his comment toward his partner's small form outlined against the oak counter beyond. "Think it was the killer?"

Adele, finally speaking to him, but still refusing to meet his gaze, called out, "Might've just been from closing. Our killer isn't stupid—methodical, careful. I doubt he would've left prints."

John glanced back at the door and fixed his eyes on the police officer waiting for them. The local hesitated, interpreting John's look, then stammered, "We'll run for prints, of course. But it doesn't seem likely."

35

John shrugged a large shoulder. "Every little clue can help."

Adele and John spent the next hour moving through the vineyard, searching various rooms and coolers, and the main office building. They even spent some time in the vineyard itself, moving amidst the plants and the dirt and the greenery. Nothing. No DNA, no usable fingerprints, no leads.

John and Adele moved back around the vineyard, finally within speaking distance once more. They paused in front of the array of windows facing into the studio, on the edge of the parking lot with the dumpsters. Adele put her hands on her hips and stared off across the fields, her eyes narrowed beneath sunlight. She said, "Our killer is careful. What are you thinking?"

John was glad she was talking to him again. "I think," he said, hesitantly, "we have a young woman kidnapped from this area, moved two miles away, then killed. That's a lot of effort. No sexual assault, no torture. Why not just kill her here? In order to kidnap her, with no witnesses, he had her on her own."

Adele also paused, standing in front of the tall glass windows. She stood beneath a wood and stone buttress, her eyes flicking along the patio, toward the glass door, and scanning the tables through the windows. She looked back at him. "Think he was a customer? Maybe stayed late?"

"Possibly."

"Maybe he showed up after hours?"

"Or he hid somewhere, waiting for her to close."

"What do you think that means?"

John grunted. "He's a devious bastard. But otherwise, I don't know. It's a strange case. Motive doesn't seem to match the murder."

Adele smoothed the front of her suit, pressing her hands against wafer-thin pinstripes stretching down the blue. She looked along the vineyard, toward the sun in the sky and blinked, wincing against the light.

She said, "I don't think fingerprints will turn up anything. He's careful. I think that's why he moved the body."

John nodded, inhaling the scent of too-sweet air. He glanced back toward the grapevines and then looked at Adele. "Still doesn't explain why he sedated them before killing. Think he's getting off on the death itself? The orgasmic rush of the light leaving their mortal eyes?" John said, quavering his voice dramatically.

36

Adele shivered. "Gross. But also, I don't know. It's possible." She hesitated, then clicked her fingers. "Hang on... Maybe we're looking at this wrong."

She moved toward the door, pushed it open—a small bell jangled overhead—and she called in, "The cash register—is it empty?"

There was a pause, the sound of murmuring, then one of the police officers moved from within, called out, "Still locked. Nothing was stolen as far as we can tell. The vineyard owner should be here soon—he'll give us a better idea."

Adele leaned dejected against the door for a moment, one elbow braced against the glass. Slowly, she allowed the door to close and she stepped back out into the dusty ground with John. "Never mind. So he *was* here for the victims. Doesn't make any sense."

"Maybe he was after the wine? Stole something, but just hid it?"

"Maybe..." Adele said, doubtfully. "We can have the owner check to see if anything is missing. He'll be able to tell us."

"You don't sound confident."

Adele shrugged. She massaged the side of her face, rubbing a flat hand over one eye in a circular motion as if to soothe a headache. "I don't know what to think just yet, John. The killer's motives don't make much sense. He killed them with as little pain as possible. The farmer it looks like he killed before he even woke up, as if he didn't want to scare the man. How does that make sense?"

John rubbed a thumb against a forefinger, wiping something sticky from the vineyard off onto his pants. "Usually they get off on fear."

Adele nodded, jamming her hands in her pockets, and then beginning to move back into the studio to wait for the arrival of the owner.

Another hour, more time wasted. Nothing to show for it. No fingerprints, no DNA, no evidence. The killer hadn't left anything behind. Why was he killing his victims? Why did it seem humane, even? Like a gentle farmer putting down an animal with as little pain as possible. Did the killer think he was performing a kindness? If so, how? John swallowed against the dry air, and then, stowing his own thoughts, he followed after his partner into the studio. Perhaps the vineyard owner would have the answers they needed.

CHAPTER SEVEN

In Adele's estimation, John had a way with words the same way a veterinarian had a way with suppositories—an intrusive, uncomfortable business that left everyone discomfited. She shot a glance toward where he stood ushering the vineyard owner into the small studio, greeting the man in French and gesturing toward the circular table around which they'd placed three chairs.

Adele had to emit a small huffing breath, steadying her nerves before adopting a pleasant expression and striding over from the oak counter to the circular table. She waited for John to usher the new arrivals to the table before saying, "Hello, are you Mr. Reber?"

A skinny, gray-haired fellow with more wrinkles than a shar-pei examined her from beneath wispy eyebrows like clouds. Next to him stood a middle-aged man and woman both dressed in neat polos and matching khakis as if they had color coordinated their outfits.

"I'm Mr. Reber," said the old man. "And this is also Mr. Reber," he said, with a flourish of his fingers toward the young man. The way the older fellow said it suggested he'd introduced their little family unit like this on more than one occasion and it gave him delight to do so.

Adele tried not to let her smile diminish in degree, but it was an effort in patience—a resource currently running on fumes.

"Good afternoon," she said, nodding to both of them in turn. Keeping her tone polite, she said, "Which of you is the owner of this establishment?"

"Both of them, darling," said the woman, stepping forward and seating herself in one of the chairs at the circular table. Agent Renee immediately fetched another two so they would have enough seats. The two local officers watched Adele's momentary confusion from where they stood by the door, displaying mild amusement.

"I see," Adele said. "You're co-owners?"

The younger man helped his father ease into another chair, and the woman answered once more. "My husband and his father have co-owned the business for the last five years. I help with operations. A terrible mess all of this—we were *ever* so fond of... what was her name

38

again? Ms. Gucci?"

"Gueyen," said Adele, this time finding despite her best efforts, her smile had slipped.

"Yes, well," said the woman, tapping perfectly manicured, rose-red nails against the smooth table beneath the window. "We do have business to continue—flew in from Italy. Rather taxing on our dear father," she said, nodding toward the older man who had finally managed to sit in the cushioned chair, and was breathing heavily from the effort.

The younger man moved dutifully to the chair nearest his father and sat as well, murmuring quietly beneath his breath, "Are you all right? Need some water?"

Before Mr. Reber could reply, though, the woman snapped her fingers toward the officers. "Water, please! If you don't mind."

"Excuse me," said Agent Renee, sitting across the table in the provided seat he'd placed earlier. "But they're not waiters. And this won't take long. We wanted to know what you could tell us about your employee, Ms. Gueyen."

The woman turned, her long—and, Adele felt certain, *fake*—eyelashes fluttering as she regarded the tall French agent. "Oh my," she said, smiling now and looking John up and down. "Mrs. Reber," she said, extending a hand in greeting. "But you can call me Margaretta."

John hid a quick smirk and shook the extended hand. "Pleasure," he said. "I'm Agent Renee. But you can call me"—he grunted as Adele elbowed him in the back—"Agent Renee," he finished, coughing.

Adele took her seat as well now. She and John sat on one side of the table, facing the strange threesome on the other.

"So you're co-owners of this place?" Adele said, deciding to start with the basics in an effort to warm the subjects.

One at a time, the Rebers nodded. The woman opened her mouth to speak again, but Adele quickly beat her to it.

"Right, and how well did you know Ms. Gueyen?" She turned to Mrs. Reber. "You said you were quite fond of her."

"Of course, dearie," said the woman, still clacking her long red fingernails against the table. "We're like a family here, after all. Little Ms. Gueyen was like a daughter to me."

Adele hesitated. "Apologies, but she was in her mid-twenties. As lovely as you are, I can't imagine you're much older than late thirties, no?"

39

The woman began to laugh, a short, baying, barking sound like a horse in heat. Adele pressed her lips firmly together, trying to pass her grimace as a thin smile.

Mrs. Reber reached out across the table, trying to press a hand against Adele's, but Adele kept her own hands folded in her lap, waiting patiently. "What a dear you are," declared the woman, pulling her hand back when it wasn't received. "I am nearly forty-two... Though, I'm known to keep up with the younger crowd," she said, wiggling her eyebrows at John. "If you know what I mean."

Mr. Reber Jr. looked to his wife, frowning. "What do you mean, Margaretta?"

She waved a hand airily as if clearing an odor. "Just a little joke, Paulo—just a joke."

Adele felt exhausted already with the exchange, and only a few moments had passed. She intentionally turned her body to face the younger Mr. Reber. His father still seemed out of it, looking over the tables, through the windows at the vineyard beyond. But the younger man seemed to be listening attentively.

"What can you tell me about Ms. Gueyen?"

"Hopefully not too much!" Mrs. Reber chortled.

This time, everyone ignored her. Mr. Reber said, "She'd only been with us for a year. Decent at her job, from what I hear. One of our older sommeliers had some complaints. But nothing that couldn't be taught."

"And this older employee—he wasn't fond of her?" said John, ratcheting up his eyebrows.

But Mr. Reber shook his head. "Oh, no—nothing like that. Andre is a good friend of the family. Can be a bit critical, if you let him have his way. But he's harmless, if that's what you're wondering."

Agent Renee nodded. "And Ms. Gueyen—can you think of anyone else who might have disliked her? Any complaints? Any comments from employees about enemies in her personal life?"

Mr. Reber sighed and shrugged. "Can't help you much there. I don't pay too much attention to the personal lives of my employees."

"Hang on, darling," said Mrs. Reber. She placed a hand against her husband's arm as if to hold him back. She said, "What about the complaint she filed? The one Andre told us about? The nasty little man who was harassing her."

Mr. Reber hesitated, then conceded with a nod. "I suppose perhaps." He looked from John to Adele. "Sometimes Ms. Gueyen would have customers make a pass at her. Part of the job, I'm afraid in this region at her age. I'm not excusing it—but it is the way of things."

John glanced at Adele, but she gave the faintest shake of her head. Inwardly, she considered Mr. Reber's words, but shelved the information as useless. A tipsy customer hitting on a sommelier didn't fit the MO. The killer was calculating, clever. Charming enough to gain Ms. Gueyen's trust before sedating her. No, this wasn't some drunken fool. Nor was it a crime of revenge or passion. The killer had struck in the Ahr region of Germany, and now in Bordeaux in France. They were looking for a practiced murderer, not a passionate buffoon.

After a few more questions, Adele flashed a look to John, which he returned. Slowly, politely, they began to extricate themselves from the situation, pushing up from the table and bidding their farewells.

Then, in lockstep, they left the co-owners of the vineyard behind them and moved back through the door, out into the afternoon now fading to evening and to the waiting car.

CHAPTER EIGHT

After dinner in the region and a taxi ride to the nearest motel, Adele was beginning to feel the weight of the day descend on her shoulders. It came in a sort of quiet prickle at first, somewhere near the base of her neck, then spreading to her spine. She winced, rolling her shoulders and shutting her eyes as John slid the keycard in the door.

She watched him, lowering her hand from massaging her neck and extending the same hand toward him expectantly.

He looked at her hand, then up at her, then back to her hand, then gave her a high five.

"No," she snapped, "my keycard, where is it?"

John paused, his mouth half open. He glanced at the card he'd just used, toward the open door on the second floor of the small motel, then back to her. A couple of tasteful pieces of simple art hung above a chocolate-wooden divider lining the hall. The carpet was surprisingly clean and the air smelled a bit of disinfectant—which, in Adele's estimation, was a significant improvement on most motels she stayed in for work.

John winced.

She stared. "You're joking—you only booked one room?"

He coughed delicately, then glanced over his shoulder again. "I thought..." he said, trailing off.

"I'm taking the bed," she said, firmly. "I hope you know that—I'm taking the bed!" Then she marched past him, into the room, snatched the keycard from his hand, and shut the door behind her, slamming it in his face.

She stood in the small motel room, glancing around. She spotted the side door leading off into a bathroom, a closed window with open blinds peering out into the street flickering with headlights. She heard a quiet tapping on the door.

"It was an honest mistake!" the voice called.

"Bite me," she retorted.

A pause. "If you'd like."

Adele rolled her eyes. "You just can't resist, can you? And there I

42

was, about to open the door and everything. Hope that hallway is comfy!"

A more insistent tapping on the door. "Adele, there are two beds! I made sure."

She glanced back at the room, noting that at least on this count he'd been right. Then, rolling her eyes and turning, she opened the door and allowed her partner to enter the room, sidling past her with the quick, coy movements of an alley cat. He winked at her as he did, and said, "My feet are very warm—don't worry."

Adele glared as he moved over to one of the beds, placing his laptop case and a small backpack next to the nightstand, and flopping onto the mattress.

"John, if I'm given any evidence as to the temperature of your feet tonight, I'll put a bullet in both of them, understand?"

For a moment, he just grinned at her, but something in her tone and gaze seemed to give him pause, because his shit-eating grin faded to a docile look of supplication and he nodded quickly, crossing his finger over his heart and extending the smallest digit. "Pinky swear," he said. "This was all a misunderstanding. If you'd like, I could go downstairs and see if they have a second room."

For a moment, Adele was tempted to make him do just that, if only to inconvenience him a bit, but then the sheer weight of the day settled on her again, and once more she reached up to rub her neck. She shook her head, sighing softly as she approached the bed and flopped onto the vacant mattress.

Adele heard the sound of an opening fridge door, and saw a sliver of orange light stretch across the length of John's outfit as he fiddled with the mini-fridge next to his bed. He withdrew a couple of small containers which, in Adele's experience, were always overpriced and under-proofed.

He wiggled one of the small containers toward her. "I'm a sommelier too," he said. "Want me to give you the tour of our fine collection?"

"John, you're an alcoholic; there's a difference."

In response, he popped the lid on one of the small containers and downed the contents, emitting a sigh of contentment. "Words hurt," he added, before peeling off the top of the second container and gulping it in one swallow as well.

Adele leaned back, closing her eyes, still in her suit and shoes.

Slowly, with sluggish motions, she kicked off her shoes, knocking them onto the ground over the edge of the bed. She watched as John downed a third bottle—likely doubling the price of the room by this point.

"John," she said, groaning, "I need you coherent for tomorrow."

"I'm always cohea-rain," John said, fake-slurring his words and adding a hiccup for good measure.

She sighed. "The real tragedy," she said, "is that you think you're funny. Could you at least hit the lights?"

"Anything for you, American Princess."

Her eyes were still closed, but she heard the sound of John hopping off his bed and taking long strides toward the other side of the room. Then the lights dimmed, and Adele was left curled in her bed, facing the large window through which streetlights still buzzed. To her surprise and appreciation, John moved over to the window as well, without being asked, and lowered the blind.

"That good?" he asked, some of the humor from his tone having faded.

"Thanks," she murmured, then pressed her cheek against the pillow, twisting until she was lying on her side.

"Ah, a side sleeper," John speculated. "I should have known."

"John," she mumbled into her pillow.

"Yes, Adele?"

"Shut the fuck up."

Evening had conceded to night, and darkness stretched into its maturity. Thankfully, John was a quiet sleeper. Adele's own mind worked restlessly, spinning thoughts keeping her awake for an hour, two... At last, muttering to herself, she went and retrieved one of the small bottles John had offered earlier. He'd left it out for her, on top of the fridge.

Tiptoeing around his bed, she moved back toward her own and tipped back the drink, wincing against the sudden bitter surge, but then flopping back into the bed. As she did, she glanced over, allowing her eyes to linger along John's form. He'd switched into sleeping clothes at some point, and the soft fabric of a T-shirt outlined against his muscled body.

Through hooded eyes, she looked him up and down, faintly wondering if the motel room had a shower.

But she was simply too tired to think in this vein for too long, and eventually, the magical elixir found in the motel room's mini-fridge did its work. Drowsiness gave way to sleep, and sleep to dreams…

…A cool hand holding hers. Quiet whispers of encouragement, murmuring, "You can do it, cara—I know you can. Don't be afraid."

Seven-year-old Adele stared at her mother, her eyes glazed in a thin film of tears.

Elise Romei, Sharp at the time, smiled sweetly at her young daughter, one hand gently pressed against her shoulder. "Do you not like the swimsuit?" she said, softly. "We can get you another if you'd like."

Young Adele just shook her head, sobbing quietly. She could feel the other children in the swimming class looking at her, and she could feel the instructors watching too. But it didn't matter. None of them understood. They wanted to throw her in that horrible pool. It was so deep, and scary, and smelled funny.

Adele hid her face in her mother's shoulder, still crying.

Elise stroked her daughter's hair, whispering softly into her ear. "You're so brave, my cara. You're so brave. You're one of the bravest people I know."

"I'm not brave," Adele said, through hiccups. Her voice cracked.

"But you are," said Elise. "Because I can see that you're scared. And yet you're still here. You haven't asked me to take you home. Do you want to go home?"

This was far too big a question for Adele to answer. She simply clung to her mother, still sobbing.

"You want me to let you in on a little secret, darling?"

Adele's head shifted up and down against where it pressed to her mother's shirt and cheek, making the soft scratching sound of hair on fabric.

"I get scared sometimes too. Very scared. Do you know what I do?"

Adele shook her head.

"Would you like to know? It's a secret, but I think I can trust you."

Little Adele could still feel the eyes in the swimming area fixed on her. She didn't want to be on the swimming team anymore. It seemed like a good idea when she'd signed up, but now she was having second thoughts. Her father wanted her to be in a sport. But Adele didn't like the water. She didn't like the smell of it, and she didn't like the way the other children all splashed around, pushing water into her eyes and nose. It stung, and she hated it.

"What secret?" said Adele.

Her mother's hand still stroked her hair, cool against her forehead, and Elise leaned in, kissing her. "When I'm scared, I think of you."

At this, Adele pushed away from her mother, looking through her tear-stained eyes. She wiped at her bleary vision and wrinkled her nose in confusion. "I scare you?"

Elise laughed. "No, but I think of you when I'm scared. Because you make me brave."

"How do I make you brave?"

Elise smiled at her daughter, affection emanating from her gaze. "Because when I think of you, I remember that there is good in the world. I remember that something makes it worthwhile. And I remember just how much I love you. Perfect love casts out fear. Something your father says. I think he heard it from a radio preacher once." Elise chuckled. "Whatever the case, when I love you, when I think of you, I don't feel so scared."

Adele tilted her head to the side just a bit, still looking at her mother. "I'm still scared."

Elise nodded. "I understand. Sometimes I can't stop being scared either. But it doesn't stay like this. I promise you. It doesn't stay like this."

The dream flitted across Adele's mind, coming in bursts and spurts and images and memories, flooding her senses. It felt like she was actually there, like she could actually smell the chlorine in the air, like she could actually feel the hot shame against her back as the others stared at her. Like she could actually feel the warmth emanating from her mother, reaching out to meet the cold of the pool air. She remembered the day, and remembered turning back and eventually trying to get in the pool. That day, she had only managed to put a foot in the water. She hadn't swum, and she hadn't even gotten in completely. But in the evening, her mother had taken her out for ice cream to celebrate. By the end of the week, Adele had tested the deep end. By the end of the month, she'd swum her first lap, and by the end of high school, she had swum competitively, winning medals for her school.

Adele smiled at the memory. *Perfect love casts out fear.* She wondered if her mother remembered Adele the last time she'd been afraid. Had that been her final thought, before she been taken from this world?

The scene shifted. Adele's eyes clenched, and she knew she was still sleeping, yet somehow, it felt different. She glimpsed tapping, dripping needles of scarlet. Blood, rolling down a path in the park. Grass stained with crimson, an outstretched hand reaching toward the roots of a tree on the side of the road. Fingers missing. A patchwork of scars, and deep gouging cuts all up and down her mother's body. Naked, abandoned, tortured to death.

Bleeding, bleeding, always bleeding.

Perfect love casts out fear.

Fear, perhaps, but the banishment didn't seem to work as well on serial killers.

And all that was left was a husk—a fleshy mass, a carved up piece of meat left in a ditch for Adele to recover.

I think of you.

Bleeding, bleeding, always bleeding.

I think of you.

***

Morning came, and with it some reprieve from the night terrors. Adele woke, glazed in sweat, finding her blankets bunched between her legs, one of the sheets wrapped in a twisting knot around an ankle, suggesting perhaps she'd tossed and turned in the night.

She breathed softly and opened her eyes, staring at the popcorn ceiling of the motel room, confronted a moment later by the pungent fragrance of cheap coffee which prompted a shiver of anticipation.

"Make me some?" she called into the morning.

"Already did," John replied. "Just keeping it warm."

She didn't quite smile, but was at least tempted to. She pushed out of the bed, wrinkling her nose at the creases in her outfit. She should have changed into sleeping clothes, but she'd been too exhausted from the previous day's events.

Sighing, and smoothing her suit, she moved over to the small table where John was sitting, a steaming mug in one hand.

"You hung over?" she asked.

He snorted. "Takes more than a couple of droplets to topple this tower."

Adele looked at him, then turned, deciding she'd rather figure out the coffee pot than Agent Renee. Sunlight dripped through the now lifted blinds, stippling her bed and the floor. John had his laptop open and was humming to himself as he scrolled through the page.

Adele sat across from him, taking a long, heavenly sip from the cheap motel-room brew.

"Anything?" she asked, her voice hoarse.

John looked at her, quirked an eyebrow. "Sleep well?" he asked, innocently.

"I don't want to talk about it," she said, all humor drained from her voice like life-blood.

John seemed to know better than to press. He waved his fingers toward the screen. "I've been trying to find a link between our victims. I think I might have it."

Adele took another sip, nearly searing her lips, but endeavoring to swallow all the same, refusing to be outdone by the beverage. "Yeah?" she said. "That's good news."

"Hopefully," he replied. He turned the computer screen so she could see. The picture displayed an old, out-of-date website with a banner depicting a cluster of grapes.

"What is it?" she said.

"The farmer—the victim in Germany. Kristof Schmidt. He grew grapes," John said, with a significant tilt of his eyebrows.

Adele now looked at him over her steaming cup and nodded slowly. "Wine, then," she said. "That's the connection. Has to be. Wine."

"A sommelier dead in France, a grape-grower dead in Germany," John said, shrugging. "A coincidence? Perhaps. But I dug a bit deeper."

Adele lowered her cup and crossed her arms now. "If I didn't know any better, I might be impressed. Did you find something?"

John smirked. "In fact, I might have. A tenuous link—but one confirmed by the Rebers." He tapped his cell phone lying on the table next to his elbow. "Amelia Gueyen used to work for a French vintner by the name of Matthias Bich—was employed at his vineyard for about a year before leaving."

"Yeah? And this vintner, what's his connection to the German farmer?"

John closed his laptop lid, looking smug. "He used to buy grapes from the farmer."

Adele actually cracked a smile now, nodding in appreciation. She studied the sunlight reflecting off the glassy table and dappling John's

48

cheeks and eyes with glowing particles. "Good work," she murmured. "No, really. It almost makes up for a night listening to your snoring."

He snorted. "I do not snore, American Princess... what is the expression? Something about a pot and a kettle?"

Adele opened her mouth in mock offense. But some of her good humor faded as she looked at the closed lid of the laptop. "Happen to have an address for this vintner?"

John tapped his phone again and pushed away from the table, getting to his feet and stretching in the shadows out of reach of the sun. "Already programmed. I'm ready to go when you are. I'll call some locals over to keep him on ice for us. They'll be able to get there faster."

CHAPTER NINE

Another squad car transported Adele and John to the vineyard of Matthias Bich an hour's drive from their motel, past Saint-Emilion on the western border of Bordeaux. As they pulled up the road, leading off the main stretch of highway, Adele couldn't help but notice this road was far better paved than the one at the Rebers' vineyard. Mr. Bich apparently took great pride in the spectacle of his establishment. The road was smooth, paved and lined with hedges and a tasteful smattering of marble statues. A few of them, perhaps predictably in Adele's assessment, shot jets of water from open mouths or tips of fingers into porcelain and marble bowls, allowing the fountains to spill back into drains and recycle the water.

Adele scanned the trimmed hedges, the ornamentation as the squad car moved along the smooth road. Ahead, the main building of the vineyard seemed to have a commercial purpose as well, displaying a title which, translated, read *Bich's Tasting and Culture.*

"Cultured," Adele murmured over her shoulder. "So much *culture.* Practically drowning in it." Once again, she'd managed to wrangle the front seat.

John grunted behind the driver's side, his gaze passing over the hedges and statues and blinking bracket lights providing tasteful illumination to the whole spectacle. Instead, he seemed to be paying particular attention to the rows of grapes beyond. "Bugs," he said. "Lots of bugs." He wrinkled his nose. "You'd think they'd have a spray or something."

The driver, another local in blue, looked into the mirror and nodded at John. "They do, sir. These insects, though, are lacewings and are not harmful to the grapes—they are called beneficial insects. Sometimes they're even pressed with the wine..." She chuckled. "Not everyone realizes just how many bugs often ended up in their Merlot."

John wrinkled his nose and glared at the vineyard now. He glanced at the mirror. "Does everyone in the area know so much about wine?"

The officer laughed and pulled the vehicle closer toward the commercial building at the end of the ornamented drive. "It's

Bordeaux, and I am French," she said, in manner of explanation, intonating the word *French* with a bit of an American accent, which Adele knew was meant to be taken humorously.

The officer's expression sobered a bit though, and she looked at Adele. "Mr. Bich is waiting for you," she said. "But he refuses to let the officers into the building without a warrant. From what I've been told, he's not being very cooperative."

"Right, thanks." Adele nodded. Then her eyes slid along the front of the large wood and glass commercial building in the heart of the vineyard toward a small gathering of people standing in front of stone slab steps. Another tasteful arrangement of multi-hued stone set in a large patio that spanned the length of the delta-shaped driveway.

The squad car pulled up behind two others, which had parked across from a blue Jaguar I-pace with chrome wheels sitting in the shade in front of a garage.

John whistled as he eyed the car, but Adele only had eyes for the gathering in front of the stone steps.

The smallest figure seemed to have positioned himself between the building and the officers in question. Any time one of the officers came too close, he would hold out a hand, blocking and shaking his head, speaking loudly. Adele rolled down the window as their car wheeled to a halt.

Over the sound of crunching dust and groaning tires, she heard the words, "...no warrant, no entry. That is final!"

She glanced over the seat at John. "I think we may have found Mr. Bich."

Together, they exited the vehicle with twin sighs of resignation, matching clicks of their locks, and synchronized slamming of their doors. The air was warm again, and Adele blinked a bit, feeling the tentative suggestions of a headache trying to make itself known. Perhaps she shouldn't have drunk that second cup of coffee before leaving the motel.

Still, there was a job to do.

She strode with John toward the gathering in front of the commercial building beneath the studio's sign. The air here now held the familiar scent of too-sweet produce and fertilizer.

Adele marched up to the small man who had his hand outstretched, blocking the three other officers who were speaking patiently with him. The man didn't seem interested in what the police had to say. He wagged a finger under the nose of a male officer and uttered a string of strong words which caused Adele to quicken her pace just a bit.

"Mighty jumpy for a vintner," John muttered next to her.

As they drew near, Adele heard the small man exclaiming. "... pay my taxes, am a good citizen. Yet you stormtroopers roll up like this? Outrageous! You'll hear from my lawyer."

"That is fine, sir," said Adele, calling out and waving a hand to catch his attention. She came to a stop on a brown stone slab set in the patio. She smoothed a couple of the wrinkles in her suit, then fixed a polite smile before acknowledging the vintner. "I assume you're Matthias Bich?"

The man turned mid-sentence, his jaw unhinged as if intent on finishing his diatribe. But then he swallowed, nearly choked on air, and rotated a full ninety degrees to refocus his ire on the new arrivals.

"And who are you?" he said. "Are you the captain I asked to speak with?"

"Captain?" John wrinkled his nose. He chuckled. "I am Agent Renee. This is Agent Sharp. DGSI. We had a few questions for you."

"DGSI?" Mr. Bich said, stunned. Not only was he quite small, but he also had a timid, mouse-like face with a weak chin and an attempt at a mustache that bordered on indecent.

The man looked at John, examining the tall, muscled agent, and instantly Adele detected a note of envious dislike.

"I was telling your goons," the man said, waving fingers toward the other officers, "no warrant, no entry." He crossed his arms over his small chest.

Adele exhaled slowly, quietly, closing her eyes for the faintest moment as if to stave off a headache. And then she moved over to the stone steps and, in John-like fashion, sat square in the middle of the step, looking up at the vineyard owner.

"Mr. Bich," she said, "we have no interest in causing you trouble. I'm happy to speak with you out here." She patted the stone slab next to her, expectantly.

For a moment, Mr. Bich just stared at her, but then, glancing uncertainly from John to the officers, he said, "You're not allowed to—"

"No one will enter your vineyard. Nor the building," Adele said, quietly. She simply wasn't in the mood to push on this front. "We're not here about your business."

The man hesitated. "You're not?"

Adele insistently patted the stone step next to her, her eyes tracing another fountain set in the side of the patio. This ornament depicted a small cherubic child with wings and a jar of wine overflowing with fountain water. She massaged the bridge of her nose and noted John watching her with an amused glint in his eye.

Eventually, Mr. Bich slowly sat on the very edge of the stone step as if preparing to lurch up and bolt at a moment's notice. Again, Adele was struck by his quick, timid twitching and his nervous swallowing.

Once he'd seated himself in front of his main building, she said, "Sir, if you don't mind, we're here regarding a Ms. Gueyen."

The man's face went pale. A poker player, he was not. He stared at her, stumbling and bumbling over words a bit before coughing dryly into a hand and looking off with a slanted gaze toward the marble fountain. "What about her?" he said, the last word practically squeaking.

Adele shot a look at John, who widened his eyes and shrugged once.

She looked back at Mr. Bich. "Sir," she said, slowly. "I can't help but notice—and I do apologize for saying so—but you don't seem to be particularly comfortable. Is there something you'd like to tell me?"

Now, he rounded on her. But the pale tinge to his cheeks was slowly being replaced by a reddish hue. He winced and stammered a bit, but then seemed to build up a head of steam, and loud enough so the officer who'd driven them, still waiting in the car, could hear, he shouted, "Whatever that little bitch is accusing me of, it never happened! She's a drama queen and a liar! That's why I fired her in the first place! There was no sexual harassment—none, zero, zilch. Understand? She's making it up. Besides," he added quickly, stammering and stuttering like someone bumbling around a toolshed in search of a weapon, "she stole from me—yes, it's true. A bottle of my finest. I had to fire her. She made up that stuff about sexual harassment when—"

"Sir," Adele said, softly. "Ms. Gueyen is dead."

She went very still, watching his expression. And again, it morphed as if his subconscious were authoring a book in real time and opening it wide over his countenance. She studied him as his cheeks turned pale again and his eyes went wide. He stared at her, jaw

53

unhinged and, for the first time since she'd arrived, seemed at a genuine loss for words.

"Dead?" he managed to gasp out.

Adele nodded once, still sitting on the dusty stone step. "Just so. We're not here about any harassment."

"I—I... I thought," he stammered, staring now from John to the other officers as if wondering if this were some sort of prank. "I thought she'd... she'd threatened to go to the cops, and... I thought... When they mentioned her name... A shame... a real shame; she was a good girl. Very fond of her. Very fond." He now rounded on the first group of officers who were watching the exchange with narrowed eyes. "Why didn't you tell me, you idiots?" he yelled. "I thought you were here about... about something else!"

Adele watched him and realized now she was detecting a note of relief in his shrill tone. Not a good sign. Relief at a deceleration of murder pegged him as an asshole, not a killer.

He looked at Adele. "Mrs. Reber," he said. "She probably did it. Probably poisoned, yes?" He looked at her gleefully. "Probably sleeping with her husband—wanted revenge. Well, am I right?"

Adele scratched at the side of her cheek, trying to peg Mr. Bich. Surely, he wasn't stupid. But at the very least, he seemed oblivious. It didn't seem to even cross his mind that he might be a suspect. Instead of correcting him on this front, though, she said, "We're looking into all leads. Just to help us narrow things down, what were you doing this Tuesday afternoon, through evening?"

If she'd thought the question would throw the vintner through a loop, she would have been sorely disappointed. He simply scoffed and waved a dismissive hand. "Fundraiser," he said. "Speaking in front of three hundred of the best vintners and sommeliers in the business." He puffed his chest importantly. "Almost made a deal, you know. With one of the big plants in America." He nodded. "Only a matter of time. You'll hear about Bich grapes world around—mark my words."

"This speech you gave," Adele said, now rubbing at the bridge of her nose. "How long did it go?"

He shrugged. "On and off for a few hours. I helped present. Then had closing remarks." He narrowed his eyes. "Just check with the Ritz Paris. I was there all day. Only came back now because you called me home!" He waved a hand toward the gathered officers.

Adele finally looked at the nearest police. "Is this true?" she said.

The man who'd received most of the abuse from Mr. Bich crossed his arms over his uniform. "Still looking into the alibi," he said. "But…" he swallowed and muttered, "department did find a plane ticket in his name that helps corroborate—"

Before he'd even finished, Adele was already on her feet, muttering darkly and stomping away, dusting off the back of her wrinkled pants and glaring at anything foolish enough to catch her eye. The little marble cherub received a particularly venomous look in its lifeless, smiling face as she marched back toward the squad car.

"A-Adele?" John called after her.

She looked over her shoulder, sun kissing her cheek, her eyes scanning the vineyard, the statuary, the wood and glass building and the four figures out front. "If the alibi doesn't check out, I'll be back," she said, in matter of warning.

But then, with an air of disgust, she slotted back into the front seat of the squad car. "Get us out of here," she muttered to the driver. And then she leaned back, closing her eyes.

She heard the door slam behind her. John's voice, "Adele, are you sure—"

"He didn't do it," she said.

"But… maybe he's lying. Maybe he had someone—"

"John," Adele said, quietly. She turned now, looking him in the eye. "You saw how he reacted. He had no clue she was dead. He was worried about harassment charges. That's it. He didn't do it. Alibi will check out." She looked back across the seat toward their designated chauffeur. "Get me out of here… please," she said. And then she closed her eyes again, trying desperately to stave off the words that had been echoing in her mind ever since she'd woken up.

I think of you… I think of you… I think of you…

CHAPTER TEN

Gabriel stepped through the sliding doors of the airport, feet on the curb, head tilted back and a smile on his handsome face. He inhaled the California air.

It was good to be home.

A few college girls passed by, tittering and giggling as their kind was wont to. When they spotted him, they all went quiet and started whispering, glancing back and shooting him a few long looks.

Gabriel smiled at the attention. A strange thing how many doors symmetrical features opened. Gates once closed, emotions once sealed would be pried apart and presented as an offering.

Then again, the only gates Gabriel was interested in didn't reside on this side of eternity.

He shifted uncomfortably, his carry-on gripped in one hand. He stepped to the edge of the curb, his other hand raised, his driving gloves clasped against his fingers as he hailed a taxi.

Of course, his name wasn't really Gabriel—but it was how he thought of himself. A testament, a claiming of an allegiance. In the past, he'd tried Loki, Lucifer, Ra, Charon. All manner of gatekeepers—those who would shuttle mortals on to eternity.

As Gabriel, though, he felt fairly certain he'd found the key. Now... the waiting, the preparing of this mortal vessel.

The handsome man on the curb outside the airport smiled in the sun, hefted his carry-on delicately, so he wouldn't disturb the precious contents, and then entered the cabin of the vehicle.

A short ride. Sonoma County. But he couldn't leave the taxi fast enough. Already, he could feel his stomach bubbling—could feel the magic slipping from his chest. The sustaining, directing source of an eternal identity. Gabriel winced against the discomfort.

Still, despite the settling discomfort, after the drive, he had the wherewithal to thank the taxi driver and tip well, before turning to enter his home. It was good to be back. He typed in the security code impatiently, his teeth now straining.

Did any of the true witnesses care?

56

"I'm hurrying!" he snapped over his shoulder. "I'm hurrying, damn you!"

Then, a flood of guilt. He froze on his doorstep and immediately dropped to a knee, tears suddenly welling in his eyes. "Please... No. I don't mean to use that word. Save me from my foolishness... Please."

Then, without even shutting the front door, he grabbed his carry-on, dragging it along as he stumbled down his hall, flicking a light and then approaching the basement door. He pulled it, listening to the quiet croak of hinges and then, still sniffling, tears on his cheeks, he tottered down the steps. Already, he was pulling the small thermos from his carry-on. Within the limit. Not much—not much at all.

A pity to leave so much pure blood back in France, but he didn't need it all. Only a taste. Only a bit to guide his path, to yield true enlightenment. Wine, like Dionysus drank, like the grapes in Eden... Wine had a god-making property. But too strong, too rich for mere mortals. Blood, similarly, was simply another type of wine. The mixture of the two caused the divine and the mortal to collide. A beautiful concoction.

But it had been so long. Even now, though, he could feel his vision clouding, the scales falling over his eyes.

Gabriel cursed at the ceiling. "Hang on," he snapped. "I'm going as fast as I can!"

The prayers were offered to no one in particular. Or, perhaps, to everyone who might listen. Anyone who might give him access to what lay beyond. He glance down at the small bottle of "cherry juice." Easy enough to smuggle—had worked before. He'd harvested abroad as well—Germany, then France. The unenlightened would never find him. This was the way of things—the way they should be.

He stumbled a bit toward the bottles against the back wall. His eyes scanned the white labels with yellow sharpie. Each of them depicting a date.

He frowned, recollecting. "How old was she again?" he murmured.

Then he lifted the small bottle of cherry juice. On the bottom, stenciled, the number "1994." His eyes flicked back toward the glinting bottoms of the wine bottles displayed against the back wall. The circular glass dots seemed like many eyes watching him, studying his movements.

With trembling fingers, he withdrew a vintage from the same year:

57

1994. Crucial they matched. Imperative, even.

Gabriel popped the cork with practiced ease, simply using his thumb and forefinger and a strong twist. Very few could uncork a bottle this way. But he'd practiced.

He poured the contents into a small tumbler sitting on the top of the wine case. Then, his fingers still shaking, he took the cherry juice and opened it. The ironlike smell of blood met his nostrils. Exhaling shakily, in a sort of orgasmic puff of breath, he poured the contents of the small container into the tumbler. Wine mixed with blood. He used his finger to swirl the contents around and around, red against red against deep red.

He smiled now. So close... so near...

He could feel the spasm wracking his body—could feel the need cloying through him desperate, searching, screaming.

"All right," he muttered. "All right. Guide me to light, accept me through the gates. Drink of my blood... I will enter!" He shouted this last part at the gray stone ceiling above. Eyes narrowed, he gripped the tumbler and then poured it into his mouth, gulping slowly at first, then faster, faster.

The taste pungent against his tongue, smooth in his throat and warm in his belly.

Some of the tremblings left, some of the anxiety lifted. He looked at himself in the small glass divider over the wine rack and beneath a bookshelf. His handsome features stared back... He looked at his hair, frowning.

Dark... no gray.

Too dark.

He growled, staring, feeling his chest heave, the rush of adrenaline that always accompanied the elixir of life. But life unto death. Life unto the next. His hair would gray, his skin wrinkle—this never scared him. This was the plan.

But it had to happen naturally. It could not be forced. To drink of a life force would spill out his own. A step at a time, a step toward eternity. His own death would be his crossing—but it needed to happen naturally. As one born without unnatural aid.

He ran his fingers through his dark hair, poked at his smooth skin, staring at his handsome features. He looked too young... He wasn't aging fast enough. He wouldn't die soon enough. He might miss it all—miss his chance. He might remain stuck this side of eternity forever!

"Damn it," he muttered, the pulse of adrenaline fading a bit now. "Damn it," he screamed, lifting his voice now.

The third vintage. He'd stuck to the recipe. The farmer had been old. The sommelier young. 1963 and 1994. The numbers of Gabriel. The code that unlocked passage. Why was he still so young? How long would he have to wait for the freedom offered?

Again. Soon. He couldn't wait. He could feel the effects fading already. The bolstering of his spirit—the rising of his soul. Not enough elixir. Not enough…

Desperately, his fingers scrambled for his pocket. Trembling again, still wearing his black gloves, he groped about for the list. Another name. Another number. Steady, steady on the narrow road unto eternity.

"Damn it!" he screamed. And then he felt a flash of guilt again. Damnation was for the others. Eternity was for the determined.

He pulled the crinkled piece of paper out, smoothing it against his gloved hand, his eyes desperately scanning now, wide, searching, hunting for the next name. The next sacrifice. The next ingredients for the elixir.

CHAPTER ELEVEN

"An email?" Adele said, staring at the side of John's face.

He grunted, shrugging one shoulder, and continued to scan his laptop screen.

Adele felt a flicker of annoyance. They were once more back in the motel just outside Bordeaux. Once again, seated at the small table near the closed door of the room they shared. The blinds on the other side of the room were opened once again, allowing the sun to stream in and reflect off the slick, glossy surface of the table and illuminate John's strong features in a soft glow.

"What does it say?" Adele said, testily.

John just shrugged again and continued to read.

She could feel her frustration mounting. Earlier, he had been annoying for constantly questioning her. Prying into her personal business. Now, though, he was annoying her by being aloof and quiet.

Or maybe you're just projecting, said a small voice in her mind.

Adele slumped petulantly in her chair, crossing her arms over her wrinkled suit. She wasn't projecting. John was projecting. What a stupid idea.

But the more she looked at her partner, the angrier she became. "What's wrong with you!" she shouted after a moment.

John, who hadn't said a word for nearly two minutes, looked at her in mild surprise. However, if she had wanted her outburst to provoke some sort of reaction, he didn't give her the satisfaction. "I said," he murmured, "I got an email from Robert. Give me a moment."

Then he returned back to scanning his computer.

Adele huffed, sighing. She felt embarrassed all of a sudden, and some of the irritation faded to be replaced by chagrin. Perhaps she was projecting. Angry at John for talking too much, angry at John for talking too little, maybe she was just frustrated with herself and the case. Faintly, she thought back to her interaction in the chocolate bar factory. The memory prompted her to wince.

"Sorry," she muttered across the table.

He didn't even seem to hear. At last, he looked up from the

computer.

Adele said, "Email was from Robert?"

John nodded once.

"That's strange," she said. "Normally he likes to call for business."

John shook his head. "You can try calling him if you want."

Adele had already attempted while John had scanned his computer. Both times, the number had gone to voicemail. "He's not picking up," she said, suppressing the cold tingle of worry scurrying down her spine. "Whatever—did he say anything useful?"

John nodded now, tapping one calloused finger against the side of his chin. "Looks like we have a suspect in the area. Robert went through a list of people who matched the MO of the killer."

Adele perked up, now uncrossing her arms and leaning across the table. "What did he find?"

John turned his laptop with a flourish and presented the image on the screen with a slight wiggle of his fingers. "Voilà," he said. "Jean Glaude, scumbag extraordinaire. Indicted on one count of sexual assault. They arrested him," John said, grimacing as he spoke, "get this, for two counts of exsanguination. Two warm ones, bled out, left in the dust. They weren't able to peg him on those charges, though."

Adele stared at John. "But they got him for the rape?"

"Looks like. This was seven years ago. He only recently got out."

Adele looked at the picture on the LED screen. It displayed a man with a short ponytail, balding on top. He had piercings all up and down his left ear, and a single hoop through his nostrils. His face wasn't anything remarkable, and he seemed to be in relatively good shape. "Looks like he's a member of Lock-up Fitness," she muttered.

"He isn't all that," John muttered. "Mr. Glaude lives about twenty minutes from here. Close enough to the sommelier."

Adele nodded slowly. "All right, worth checking out. What did they have tying him to the exsanguinations?"

John shrugged a shoulder. He glanced back at the screen, rotating the laptop just a bit and causing it to squeak against the glossy surface of the table. He read a moment longer, then said, "Only circumstantial. Couple of witnesses saw a man fitting his description enter the building. Security cameras spotted his vehicle in the area. But nothing enough to convict. He skated on those charges."

Adele pushed away from the table, getting to her feet for a moment, and she felt a flicker of worry which had nothing to do with

61

the case.

"Did Robert say anything in the email? Is he doing okay?"

John gave her a musing look. "Didn't see anything. He just sent the email. Why?"

Adele breathed heavily. She reached into her pocket, pulled out her phone, and went to the most recently dialed numbers. She tried it again and waited a few moments. After a second, a buzz, and then an annoying, clinical voice. Voicemail.

She cursed and stowed her phone. "It's nothing," she muttered. "Come on; let's go check out Mr. Delightful."

John flashed a thumbs-up. "Our squad car should be patrolling the area. Just let me get my jacket."

CHAPTER TWELVE

It was the same officer who had driven them to Mr. Bich. The policewoman pulled the squad car up to the curb outside the small French public housing complex.

She nodded through the window, toward the dirt-stained once-white building. "That's the address," she murmured. "Sure you don't want backup? This isn't exactly a hospitable area."

Adele jerked a thumb over her shoulder from where she sat in the front seat once more. "That's my backup," she muttered. "We'll be fine."

John, the indicated party, chuckled quietly to himself as he pushed out the back door. Adele followed, and the two of them stepped into the afternoon. The sun was playing peekaboo behind some clouds and above, sitting on a couple of telephone wires, two blue-feathered birds darted around, chirping and chasing each other.

Save the birds, the rest of the area seemed in disrepair. The buildings themselves were stained gray, the driveways cracked and scattered with stone. The grass was sheared too close, as if the tenants couldn't be bothered to mow frequently, and wanted to put off the chore as long as possible.

A row of slotted mailboxes with locks sitting on the curb boasted the addresses for nearly fifteen of the units surrounding the street.

"Mr. Scumbag lives up here?" she asked.

"One-fifty-five," John muttered. "No telling what the idiot will do. Better be careful."

Adele nodded, and together with John, she moved up the sidewalk, toward the dilapidated building, and through the front glass door that led into the small entry. A row of buzzers was set in the wall next to her.

She tried the handle, but it was locked. John reached across her and slid his finger down all the buttons, stepping back a second later.

There was a pause, then a crackle of a voice asking, "Who is it?"

John and Adele didn't reply. John ran his fingers down the buttons again. A few seconds later, the door buzzed. John smirked, pushed open the door which creaked on rusted hinges, and moved into the small, cramped space in the atrium of the building.

The air here smelled of mold and cigarette smoke concealed poorly by cologne. The stairwell itself was sagging, a portion of the wall bloated from water damage.

Adele wrinkled her nose. "Doesn't seem like our scumbag extraordinaire is too concerned with hygiene."

John shrugged. "Maybe he doesn't have a choice."

Adele paused for a moment, and nodded. "Good."

The two of them moved up the stairs, reaching the end of the long hall.

"One-fifty-five?" she said.

John maneuvered ahead of her, his hand on his hip, his weapon visible beneath the tucked edge of his shirt.

Adele put her own hand near her waist. She wasn't nearly as quick off the draw as John, so she unhooked her holster, deciding one could never be too careful. They moved down the hall past 150... 151... 152... A couple doors later, next to another portion of wall where the wallpaper was peeling from more water damage, beneath a particularly impressive black mold stain, Adele came to a halt.

"Door's open," John muttered.

Adele stared at the crack in the entryway and pushed.

The door creaked, but then went taut. It was stuck on a chain. But a thin glimmer of flickering light, as if from a TV, emanated from within apartment 155.

Adele pressed against the door, feeling the cold of the metal against her cheek; she glanced along the gap, into the apartment. The angle of the slightly ajar door gave her a long look into a kitchen crowded with piles of bottles, a scattering of newspapers on top of the stove, and a sink full of dishes, with a couple of flies flitting around beneath a window that stared out into a side alley. Adele wrinkled her nose.

She tapped her fingers against the door; no response.

"Sounds like he's home," John murmured.

The TV continued to blare and buzz.

Adele raised her voice. "Mr. Glaude, are you in there?"

No answer.

"Mr. Glaude?" she said, louder now. A slow prickle spread down her spine.

64

No answer. She tapped even more insistently against the door until her knuckles practically bruised against the metal.

"Adele," John said, sharply.

She felt another tingle across the back of her neck, and looked at her partner.

John was pointing toward the microwave set in one of the cupboards. The glass surface of the door reflected the glow from the TV, and then something on the floor.

She strained, trying to discern the shape displayed in the glass. Then she realized what it was and went suddenly very still, her eyes widening.

A body lay on the ground in front of the TV, face down.

"Get back," John said, sharply.

Cursing, her arms prickling with goosebumps, she stepped aside, her weapon already springing out of her holster. John took two lunging steps and shoved hard; there was a splintering sound as the chain pulled from the door itself, cracking against the wood. The chain now dangled, with a fragment of the frame still stuck to its side. The door slammed open, and Adele and John stumbled in, weapons raised.

"DGSI!" Adele shouted.

Both of them pointed their weapons around the room, across the disgusting kitchen, into the small, dingy, hazy apartment. The air smelled of skunk weed and mold.

She spotted an overflowing trashcan next to two bags with blue ties adjacent to the bin. She turned toward the TV and the corpse, her heart hammering.

Except, it wasn't a corpse.

The body was still moving, emitting low, gurgling sounds and huffing breaths.

John hesitated and then grunted. A second later, scanning the scene, he slowly stowed his weapon. "Mr. Glaude?" John asked, some of the energy fading from his tone.

John took a couple of steps toward the snoring man lying prone on the ground. He had a bottle of wine clutched in his hand, his lips sucking on it. Adele noticed another couple of bottles scattered beneath the counter. She leaned down, poking at one, listening to the glassy, rolling sound as it slid across the tiles.

"John, this one's from the same vineyard where Ms. Gueyen worked," she said.

John snatched a big handful of the man's hair—balding on top, but a long ponytail. Adele spotted many earrings through the man's ears. John gripped the greasy hair, winced in disgust, but then lifted the head.

The man continued to snore, his eyes sealed, his jaw hanging, a thin trail of drool spilling down onto his fingers. Above him, the TV was playing a pornographic film.

"I think we found our princess," John said. And then he tapped the bottle, picked it up, and wiggled it. "And here's her glass slipper."

Adele wrinkled her nose, moving over to John, and slowly, with his help, lifting Mr. Glaude.

"Guess we'd better take him down to the station. More than one of these bottles is from Ms. Gueyen's workplace—he likely knew our victim."

Together, John and Adele endeavored to wake their suspect, at the same time trying to keep their distance for the sake of hygiene, while simultaneously reaching for handcuffs.

CHAPTER THIRTEEN

Nina Wagner hefted the small brown box. She tucked her tongue inside her cheek, shouldering the container, and wincing as one of the bags of sugar nearly toppled over the edge. She resisted the urge to curse, blinking beneath the sun just outside the small wine-making store, Artisan's Supplies. She looked over her shoulder, embarrassed, wondering if anyone was watching her struggle. Then, huffing a bit, she tottered, one step at a time, barely able to see over the box toward her car.

She felt her purse swinging off the strap on her arm, dangling low. If anyone opportunistic came by, she'd be helpless to prevent them from snatching it.

Puffing and huffing, she reached the back of her small sedan and placed the box on the lid of the trunk. Then she exhaled, hands on her hip as she gathered her breath. She glanced back toward the shop and noticed one of the clerks smiling at her. She gave a little wave. Nina smiled back and waved in return. Today was a good day. Far too warm and bright and full of hope to be filled with anything close to resentment. Besides, everything in that little box of hers was just the ingredients for the next best vintage in the area—ingredients to her future. Perhaps even the future of her children and their children. In her early forties, she had heard from many how it was quite late in the game to be getting into wine-making. But Nina had never been one to back down from a challenge. She'd spent the last couple of years studying the craft, practicing, perfecting. And now, she felt certain she'd reached the perfect blend.

All that remained was getting these new appliances into the studio. She looked at the box on top of the trunk, and then toward the lock.

"Oh dear," she muttered.

The items in the box needed to be in the trunk, but the box held the lid shut. She sighed, and resigned herself to another embarrassing shuffle. She grabbed the box, lifting it, and slowly lowered it to the ground. But just then, the strain from too many items broke through the side of the box. The corner gave out, and a flap of brown dangled down. One of the glass decanters fell, smashing on the gravel.

She moaned and lowered the box completely now, quickly, so that nothing else would fall through the gap. She glanced back toward the clerk through the shop's window, and realized that she was now looking pointedly away. Clearly, replacing the smashed item was off the table.

"Excuse me," said a voice from behind her, "are you okay?"

Nina turned, and raised an eyebrow. A very handsome man was walking toward her. A bit of his charm was lost on her, of course. Nina hadn't been with a man in twenty years. Like wine, everyone had their taste, and hers tended to veer toward a sweet Moscato rather than the expected Rosette. Still, she could appreciate beauty, and this fellow certainly had it in spades. His eyes were a marvelous blue, and his smile, set in that masculine jawline, looked like something off a billboard.

"Hello," she said, gasping and wheezing a bit. "It's nothing, nothing. Just a little accident. I'll be fine."

He leaned against a van, his shoulder pressing against the cool metal. "Oh," he said, "want me to give a hand?"

She waved away the offer, still bent over. He seemed friendly enough, and there didn't seem to be judgment in his eyes as he watched her try to wrangle her perforated box of wine supplies.

"You're an amateur or professional?" he asked.

She looked up. "You partake yourself?"

He smirked. "You could say that. You have all the right ingredients, but it looks like you broke your decanter. I actually have a spare one. If you'd like."

She stared at him and nearly felt a tear of gratitude reached the corner of her eye. "Truly? I'd replace it, but I don't think they'll accept the broken return. You have an extra?"

He nodded, still smiling. "Certainly. Here, come. My car is just over this way. I always carry an extra."

She glanced at the box and then give it a little kick, partly to stow it under her car in the shade as much as possible, but also in a gesture of resentment. The box could wait. She followed after the nice man, stepping along in his shadow. They moved around the side of the store toward the parking lot behind the building. Fewer cars were parked here, and a row of dumpsters lined the wall, obscuring the view from the rest of the parking lot.

It was as she passed the dumpsters that Nina paused for a moment. Then again, if the man had wanted her purse, he could've just snatched it earlier. And now, as she moved with him, she felt caught between indecision. She really did want that decanter.

"Don't worry," he said, genially, waving, "I'll just get it for you if you'd like."

She paused, but then felt silly and pushed aside the fear. "No, no. Here, thank you. It's so very kind of you. I won't make you carry it. I really, really do appreciate it. Do you also—"

She trailed off as she reached the back of a white van. The man opened the door. Inside, there was an array of tubing, a metal pole pressed from the bottom of the floor to the ceiling. An IV bag dangled with plastic tubing. She wrinkled her nose.

"What's that?" she said, curiously.

The man was looking at her now, a strange gleam in his eye. And then, as she stared, he burst forward in the flurry of rapid motion. Moving fast, far too fast. He covered the distance between them before she could even shout out. Athletic, feral, wild. His eyes pulsed, no longer so much blue as a violet blaze. His hand shot out, and her scream was caught in a gurgle. His thumb pressed hard, with practiced ease, against something in her throat. Her eyes rolled back. Dark splotches across her vision. No more vision. No more thought.

Her consciousness fled.

***

Gabriel breathed heavily, closing the back of the van door and looking quickly over his shoulder. He scanned the side parking lot next to the old shops.

No one was watching. People rarely did.

Gabriel rounded toward the front of the vehicle, got in the front seat, and glanced over his shoulder toward the back. The old, middle-aged woman was lying on her belly. She was a bit round. But then again, he wasn't looking for ideal health. He was looking for life. And life could only be found on the other side of death. But if one cheated, the gatekeepers would block entry. Meticulous, careful, a constructed path—he had to follow it.

He pulled out of the parking spot, his breathing steadying a bit. He stretched his shoulders and pressed his hands against the steering wheel. He'd practiced unarmed combat for years. Years as a child, then an adult. He'd always known it would serve him one day. He had sensed destiny even at a young age.

And of course, he couldn't possibly sedate the donors. It would spoil their blood. Taint the elixir. Such sacrilege would never be forgiven. Damnation would be complete.

He glanced back in the mirror, looking at the form of his unconscious livestock. Her body jiggled a little, the extra poundage wobbling as the car moved down the road and up the side street.

The van wasn't even his. His alibi was in place already. Hunting this close to his home had never been part of the plan. But perhaps that's why it wasn't working. Perhaps that's why his hair had yet to gray. Perhaps that's why the wrinkles hadn't yet set in. The natural progression of the elixir, leading him through death to life. Perhaps he'd been operating in fear. And fear would never yield good results. No.

He swallowed, glancing back. He'd picked the perfect spot nearby, but far enough that no one would watch.

The tires spun, and the van pulled away, along the gray roads, between forest paths in Sonoma County. Wine region. Close to the city of fallen angels, but far enough away that hope remained.

***

The needle in her arm. The lifeblood spilling, drops at a time, pooling through the tube into the bag. He unlatched the small toolbox sitting next to the IV stand. They had come to a halt. In a forest, an old preservation. Nearby, he knew summer camps would take place. But the camps wouldn't be in session for a while longer. They would have all the privacy they needed. He would have the time required.

He watched the steady stream of red, smiling as he did. Such a beautiful sight; he wondered if this was how Picasso felt when melding colors together on his palette.

The woman began to shudder. She looked up, one eye blearily fluttering.

He cursed and lashed out again, his arm like a piston, his thumb slamming into her neck, cutting off the supply of the carotid artery.

She collapsed again, unconscious once more. He didn't want them to suffer. There was no sense in that. But he needed more this time. Not

70

just the small amount he could smuggle in. More, far, far more.

One IV bag filled. He reached over and began to replace it with the next one. He would take every last ounce he could find. It was necessary, an important step.

"Accept the sacrifice," he murmured, quietly.

He needed more. Much, much more.

But as he fiddled with the next IV bag, the tubing slipped. The back of the van was cramped. He was used to more space. The tube fell, and red liquid began spilling, pooling in the bottom of the van. He cursed and quickly yanked it up, trying to put it back in. But this time, he pulled the tube out from the needle. Blood began pouring down the woman's arm, sliding along the van's floor, getting between the cracks in the plastic, sliding beneath the back seats.

He huffed now, looking desperately through the van windows, the doors open. No one nearby. Just trees and leaves to witness the frailty of this poor, fractured vessel.

"Forgive me," he murmured. "Forgive me."

He scrambled, desperately scooping some of the blood, looking at his fingers and wincing against the sudden shiver of pleasure.

Scrambling fingers, he reattached the hose, pressing it to the needle, and led the line back into the second IV bag. He would have to be more careful. More careful, or he could spoil the recipe entirely. The list would check out. Nina had been on the list. He just needed more. So very much more.

A slow, cool breeze swirled through the back of the van, wafting across his cheeks, over the fallen, unconscious form of the amateur winemaker. It was all going to be over soon. It had to be. But he was patient. He was faithful. Even if it took months, he would walk the path set before him. He would finish the race well.

CHAPTER FOURTEEN

"I don't like you, and you smell funny; I just want to get that out of the way to begin." John looked straight into the eyes of the man he was insulting, and gave a slight little shake of his head.

Mr. Glaude scratched his cheek, his chained hands rattling a bit. He looked from John to Adele and snorted a bit, swallowing before saying, "Is he allowed to talk to me like that?"

Adele shrugged. "He talks to me like that. Not really much I can do about it."

Jean Glaude looked at Adele. His hair was still pulled back in a ponytail, and the bald spot across his head shimmered with sweat beneath the pulsing LED lights above. This interrogation room was nicer than most of the ones Adele had been in. Much like everything in this region, comfort seemed to matter. Even the chairs were cushioned, and the table, to her astonishment, wasn't even metal. The handcuffs as well had padding on the inside.

John was leaning back in his chair, hands crossed behind his head, seemingly content he'd said everything he wanted to.

Adele regarded their suspect. "I can keep asking you, if you'd like. But we know you knew Ms. Gueyen."

"No clue who that is." He spoke in a voice that suggested a permanent slur. Or, perhaps, permanent inebriation. He'd had enough bottles in his apartment to floor a grizzly bear.

"You don't look in a very good state," she said, bluntly.

He raised an eyebrow at her, as if the hairs were trying to escape up toward his bald spot. "This is how they teach you to speak to people?" He just shook his head, looked away. "You're trying to bait me. I'm not stupid."

"Where did you get those bottles?"

He looked at her, held her gaze, and then, some of the slur fading from his voice, he enunciated, "From Chateau Bordeaux. Maybe even this Ms. Gueyen. I don't know. I'm from Bordeaux, and I'm French. We drink wine. That's not a crime."

"I read your file, it's very interesting. Not a particularly pleasant read. What would your mother think in Cologne if we read it to her?"

She seemed to hit a nerve. He glared at her. "What does my mother have to do with this? Have some respect."

She shrugged. "I wonder if your victims felt the same way. When you forced yourself on them."

The man snorted. "I didn't murder anyone."

John said, "That's not what your file suggests. Seems like you got away with it, but you definitely murdered those two college kids nearly a decade ago. You were seen."

The greasy, half-drunk felon muttered, "Just like you folks; always pinning something on those who've already serve their time. I paid for my crimes. Just let me live my life."

"Happy to," John said. "Long as you do the same for others. Then again, maybe I'm not so happy to. You know what, I'm not sure I even care if you did it." He lowered his voice, and in a conspiratorial whisper, he added, glancing at Adele, "Honestly, I'm tired. I want to go home. Let's just pin it on him. The judge will believe us. Send him away for life. Keep that stink away from others."

"Hang on—look. This Ms. Gueyen. Really, no clue who that is. I've been on a three-day bender," he retorted. "I don't even remember where I keep my pants."

John was staring at the man across the table. He spoke in a low voice. "I don't even care that you're a rapist. I don't care that you're probably a murderer. I just don't like how you look. It's the smell. It's your eyes. I used to put people down just for looking at me the way you do. It'll be nice to find you, one day, outside the precinct, just the two of us. My partner here," he glanced at her, and tilted his head to indicate, "she's nice. I'm not."

"John, relax," Adele murmured softly. But her partner ignored her.

Mr. Glaude was staring, his mouth half open. The threat was heavy in the air, and the attempted intimidation seemed to stretch between them. His handcuffs rattled a bit, but then Mr. Glaude seemed to snap out of the spell, as if he remembered where they were. He snorted, and actually spat now, onto the table, some of the droplets getting on John's hands.

Mr. Glaude returned John's smirk. "You think you're the only one that knows how to have a good time? You think you're the only one that has played with people's insides before? You don't scare me; you're a poser! Those two bodies, I didn't do it," he added quickly.

73

"Never touched a hair. What you're accusing me of now, never did it either." But then his face broke into a skeletal leer, a smile stretching his cheeks like taffy. "If I did, though, I would've liked them big. Big and stupid, like you. I would've used a small little knife, rusty, blunt. Tear the skin. Maximum pain. They'd squeal like a bunch of little stuck piggies. Ever heard a pig squeal like that before?" he said, still leering at John. "Maybe you have a sister, a mother, or," he shuddered in delight, "a little daughter." He gasped, making a sort of orgasmic sound that made Adele clench her teeth. "I would spend so much time enjoying their company. Not that I ever did. But, one can imagine," he said, and after finishing, he leaned back, shoulders pressed against the cushioned chair, hands limp against the table. The thin veneer of spit still streaked the table.

John went suddenly cold. Through hooded eyes, the eyes of an actual killer, he looked at Adele. "Sounds to me like he's saying he did those murders from last decade. Think that's a confession?"

Adele sighed. John's tactics were never protocol, but often effective. "Certainly enough for a judge to want to take another look at his case. I'll make sure to tell the locals."

Adele looked at her partner and then glanced back at the felon. "I think you did those other two. The ones you got away with. Now, you've been recently released, and one of the workers at a vineyard you visit was also killed, also exsanguinated."

The man across the table was now shaking his head wildly, his ponytail shifting back and forth. "You're insane," he said. "Absolutely insane. I didn't do it."

Adele's phone began to buzz.

She frowned, her eyes narrowed. She hated when she was interrupted when they had a suspect rattled. John had played his cards perfectly. Adele was not someone averse to mercy. She didn't consider herself a bloodthirsty person. Even someone like Mr. Glaude, in her opinion, could be redeemed. She didn't give a damn if no one else agreed with her. There were some, like Agent Paige, who would scream at her just for holding the thought. Adele wasn't interested in vengeance or revenge, or making people pay. She was interested in solving crimes. But if he really had gotten away with two murders, that meant justice hadn't found him yet. Redemption or not, the law spoke first. And in this case, she thought, perhaps it had forgotten its lines. It was up to her to provide them. If he had killed before, perhaps he had killed again. He had the opportunity, the motive.

The phone continued to buzz, and she fished it out. She held up a finger toward John, then turned and moved to the door, pushing out into the hall. The hall was empty; the small department hadn't provided anyone to guard the door. This suited her just fine. Adele preferred working without much oversight.

Then again, on the subject of oversight, her eyes widened at the name on the screen. She cleared her throat and tried to look less tired and haggard. She answered and said, "Ms. Jayne, a pleasure to hear from you."

The face on her screen was of a woman with a neat and tidy appearance. She had white hair, trimmed and combed, and a very thin application of makeup across a sincere, round face. She was a bit heavier than most field agents, but had an intelligent gaze, peering out from behind her glasses.

In crisp, curt tones, suggesting a mastery of a language not her native tongue, Miss Jayne said, "Agent Sharp, the pleasure is mine. I wish I could be calling you under better circumstances, but something has come up."

Adele frowned. She half glanced back toward the door closing behind her and sealing the interrogation room. "Something else? What?"

Ms. Jayne pursed her lips, her eyes practically seeming to pop out of the screen, seeing Adele and holding her gaze. "A third body. The same MO."

Adele frowned. The suspect had been in cuffs, and when they'd found him he'd been in no state to kill anyone. Perhaps, though, it had been from earlier. Maybe he'd done it, and raced back to his apartment to get drunk as an alibi.

"Where?" she said.

"You're not going to like it," said Ms. Jayne. "California."

Adele stared. She stammered, "But, but that's impossible. He couldn't have possibly." She trailed off, glancing toward the sealed door, then back to her phone. Then, in a weakened voice, she said, "When?"

Ms. Jayne didn't blink, her tone precise. "This morning, behind a small winemaker's shop in Sonoma County. I assume you're familiar?"

"Are... are you sure?" she stammered. "What were the conditions?"

75

Ms. Jayne responded, speaking the gruesome details without batting an eyelid, ever the consummate professional. "Her body was found off a stretch of highway in the Sonoma Valley in California. The woman was seen leaving a wine-making supply store—her car is still there. She was found with her throat cut, but almost no blood at the scene. She bled somewhere else, then was dumped on the road—nearly completely drained."

Adele could feel her hand curling, forming a fist. This was the worst part of any investigation—a false trail, leading to another body. She swallowed, breathed, unclenching her fist. "The locals—they find anyone?"

Ms. Jayne shook her head in one swift motion. "No trail," she said.

Adele winced. "Are we sure it's not a copycat?"

Ms. Jayne shook her head again. "We were intentional to keep a lid on the details of this case for that very reason. A globe-trotting murderer doesn't need help from the media. I've already spoken with Agent Grant from your old field office. She's happy to host you and provide whatever is needed so Interpol and DGSI can correspond with the FBI."

Adele shuddered and nodded once.

"I need you and Agent Renee back stateside."

Adele closed her eyes, focusing, then nodded. "Not a problem at all, ma'am. Back to the states it is."

"And Adele…" Ms. Jayne's normally stoic expression twitched. "This one is becoming a headache. The killer is moving too fast— across countries. If this gets out, given current political climates in two of the countries, it could spell disastrous. Understand? Executive Foucault should have already spoken to you."

"Political how?"

"Let me worry about that. You worry about catching this guy— *fast*. Understand? We can't have another death."

Adele nodded and then lowered her phone, clicking it, placing it back in her pocket. For a moment, she just stood in the cool hall, the empty area across from the closed interrogation room door. There went that theory. It couldn't have possibly been Mr. Glaude. He was a scumbag, and by the sound of things, a scumbag who had gotten away with murder. But not this murder. She went to the door, tapped, and opened. John looked out at her from where he'd been taunting the felon by the looks of things. Mr. Glaude looked even more scared than when

76

she'd left.

But when John spotted her gaze, he frowned. "What's wrong?"

She just shook her head and gestured at him. He paused, then nodded significantly toward their subject. "You're sure?" he said.

Adele said, stiffly, "Not him."

John now turn fully, swiveling in his chair and glaring at her. "Hang on, are you—"

"John, it's not him. Come."

John got to his feet and gave one last long look at Mr. Glaude. "You have my word," he said, in a slow, ominous voice, "the judge will take another look at your case."

Then he stomped out of the room, shutting the door hard behind him. In the hall, he rounded, facing Adele. "What?" he demanded.

Adele looked up at him, crossed her arms, and stood with one foot just ahead of the other. "I just got a call," she said. "Third body." She filled her partner in on the details, and by the end, some of the anger seemed to have faded from John's expression to be replaced by a quiet resignation. He shrugged, staring at her. "What now?"

"Now, we go to America."

CHAPTER FIFTEEN

Badgers kept burrows, lions their dens, and federal agents had planes. Once more, Adele pressed her shoulder against Agent Renee, shifting a bit to try to find a more comfortable position. No time for first class this flight—haste was of the essence. Already, they were halfway across the ocean, soaring from one continent to the next as if it were as simple as casting flowers to the wind.

For Adele, the journey was a familiar one. She glanced at her partner, though, and vaguely wondered how John might fare in the States. He'd often teased her about being from America, as the French were wont to do, but now, both of them were on the hunt.

Sonoma Valley—not far from where Adele had settled while working for the FBI. She'd visited once or twice before. Adele had already been over the case details and now she could see them flickering across her mind's eyes as she adjusted, sliding her shoulders against the rough, uncomfortable backrest of the economy seat. Above, the nozzle of cool air wasn't working, and her small, personal TV set into the seat before her wouldn't turn on, no matter what she tried.

To add insult to injury, the air smelled a little bit of a dirty diaper, and every few minutes she could hear the quiet mewling of the child from two seats over who had likely provided the fragrance.

Still, she'd suffered worse. Then again, not *much* worse.

Next to her, John was stiff as a log, sleeping, his head pushed against the plastic cover surrounding the pill-shaped window. The visor was open, displaying clouds and the long stretch of the airplane's wing, the giant engines humming and propelling them through the air.

After another series of futile readjustments, which ended in more discomfort, Adele finally closed her eyes, trying to think. The idea of falling asleep as John had was far too great an aspiration and she didn't dare tempt herself with such false hope, but at the very least she hoped she could rest her eyes.

And, if the steady stream of odor from the child in 33B continued, she might request a couple of ear plugs for her nostrils to rest those as well.

As she tried to settle, the details of the case spun through her mind. A third victim—middle-aged, female, this time in California. Three countries, three victims, different ages, different genders. All of them connected to wine somehow. One, a grape farmer, the other a sommelier, and this last one an amateur winemaker. The woman's car had been discovered outside a wine-making supply store. Abandoned, a small box of purchased items left discarded on the ground, a shattered decanter left scattered across the asphalt. Had the killer ambushed her? Had he snuck up from behind?

Adele winced and readjusted, turning a bit to press her cheek against the headrest and her rear against John's upper thigh. At least no one had booked the seat between them.

The thoughts didn't end at the case though. Other pulses of consideration haunted her, tempting her with various smatterings of despair. Loudest of all was a simple consideration: What if they were chasing this guy around the world just to give him the time he needed to flee somewhere else? A perpetual game of cat and mouse where the mouse was always three steps ahead.

Bodies would fall, agents would follow, and the killer would escape.

They couldn't keep doing this. They needed something—a lead, an idea, a clue, something to narrow the gap.

Adele could feel a bit of sweat now forming on her forehead and she opened an eye, glaring angrily up at the malfunctioning air nozzle. She sighed as discomfort settled complete. She stretched, reaching up and twisting at the nozzle a few more times—but no air, no luck.

Adele's eyes lowered and she glanced across the aisle, perhaps in search of something to envy—some passenger comfortable beneath a stream of air watching their working TV.

Instead, though, her eyes skimmed over a couple of sleeping passengers and a large man who took up two seats, and landed on a small girl.

The girl was watching Adele, her nose scrunched in curiosity.

Adele smiled and mimed fanning her hand at her face and then sticking her tongue out and panting like a dog.

The young girl giggled, but then returned her attention to the item in her hand. Adele went still all of a sudden, her silly expression fading. The young girl had a small Carambar beneath her fingers. She was rolling it along the table, half-unwrapped.

When she noticed Adele staring, the child extended the candy, offering it across the aisle.

Adele shook her head and exchanged a small smile in return. She turned away from the young girl now, troubled, her mind spinning again. Carambars. The only lead she had in her mother's case. A memory in a memory buried in a coffin of memories.

She swallowed and winced, trying to focus. Derailing now wouldn't help anything. Try as she might, though, Adele couldn't focus. Like watching a projector playing bits and pieces of one movie, then switching to another, then back.

She opened her eyes again, glancing toward the little girl. She was sucking on a straw, a small box of juice pressed and crushed beneath her small hand. The girl no longer seemed to notice Adele's attention. But Adele, for her part, stared at the juice box.

Her mouth went dry. The heat from the failed nozzle above had also caused her to be parched.

Wine...

Why wine?

She stared as a small little red splotch appeared on the corner of the young girl's lip. She reached up, wiping it away, then with a sucking sound suggesting she'd emptied her juice box, she pushed against her sleeping father's form next to her, whispering for another.

Wine. Red wine.

That's what the amateur had the ingredients to make. Some sort of red wine... The sommelier had served something to the killer... a single glass—only carrying the girl's prints though. But the glass... it had red wine in it. Just a bit, only a small amount remaining, but wine all the same. Again, red.

Why wine?

Adele fished her phone from her pocket, frowning. She cycled to her settings, connected to the airplane's Wi-Fi, then, desperately, focused, she scanned to the file John had sent her the day before. Her eyes flicked down the device, searching...

***

John jerked up, blinking and wincing against the buzzing light emanating from the seat next to him.

"Adele?" he grunted.

80

She looked up, her face haggard, but her eyes wide with excitement. Her phone was bright and luminescent against a backdrop of a mostly quiet plane now. The lights had been dimmed and even most the personal TVs were off.

John grunted. "What are you doing?"

She waved her phone at him, nodding to herself, then, as if wanting to include him in the joy of the gesture, nodding to him as well. "I found it," she murmured. "I found it."

John raised an eyebrow, turning fully now to face her. He reached up and rubbed at the side of his forehead, feeling the ridge lines where his skin had indented from pressing into the plastic window. Ahead, the chair had leaned back, scrunching his long legs. He wished he'd insisted on the aisle seat. But also, he got sick on planes and windows helped. He hated flying, though he'd be damned if he ever let Adele find out. He'd never hear the end of it.

"Do you know what type of grapes the German farmer cultivated?" she said, maintaining somewhat of an effort to keep her voice down.

Judging by a couple of nasty looks from the passengers across the aisle, she failed in this endeavor. John returned their glares, and they looked away, pretending as if they'd been stretching. He glanced back at his partner.

"Grapes? No."

"Exclusively," she said, "he cultivated Spatburgunder."

"Bless you."

"No," she snapped. "They were red grapes, John."

He nodded slowly. "Are... are you all right?"

"John," Adele snapped. "Listen—he cultivated red grapes. The American victim was creating red wine. The French victim had red wine in the bottom of her glass. Those splotches on the wall in the kill room... also red!"

John had never considered himself a particularly stupid man. But sometimes, around Adele, he wondered if he were slow on the uptake or if she were simply confounding in the worst way possible. "Blood is red," he supplied helpfully.

"John... Yes, it is," Adele said. "The wine is red, and the blood is red. And all of them are connected to red wine. But also, blood was taken—exsanguinated. Do you understand?"

And, to his near astonishment, he did. John gaped. "You—you

81

don't think he's drinking it, do you?"

Adele shrugged and pocketed her phone once more, nodding to herself again.

"Hang on," he interjected. "He's not a vampire, is he? You're aware this is the real world, right?"

"Well... sort of. I've been researching people who drink blood."

"Vampires." John nodded.

"No... People who actually do this, not just on TV."

John paused for a respectable amount of time, then volunteered, "Vampires."

"Not vampires, John. Sanguinarians. They drink other people's blood—for a variety of reasons. I think our guy might be one. He drains them, John. This connection to wine, red wine, and the missing blood. It can't be a coincidence, can it? What if he's not just bleeding them— but also drinking it? At least some of it?"

John stared at her, slack-jawed. He scratched at his chin. "How... how exactly does that help us?"

At this, Adele sighed and looked dismayed. "I don't exactly know. It's not really a lead..." But then she added, "It is a motive, however. It might help... Why these three victims specifically? Why across different countries? Don't you see—if he's drinking their blood, there's *a reason* behind it. That's our connection. That will bring us to him."

John gave a soft little grunt. "I hope so. Now, Adele... Sleep. You look like a vampire yourself."

It was testament to just how tired she was that instead of retorting, Adele actually closed her eyes, leaned back, and began to breathe slowly, doing her best to follow his advice.

CHAPTER SIXTEEN

Adele and John scanned the cars slipping through the roundabout outside the terminals. After a few moments, Adele tipped her head toward an unmarked gray sedan with tinted windows. The front driver's side window was lowered, and she spotted a familiar face.

As the car rolled to a stop in front of the curb where the two agents from France stood, Adele called, "Hey, Sam, good to see you!"

The young man in the front seat smiled in return and unlocked the doors, gesturing for them to enter. He spoke rapidly, rattling off, "Need help with the luggage?"

John wrinkled his nose in a distasteful expression, like someone moving from a cool air-conditioned room out into searing summer heat. He'd never much liked speaking in English, and Agent Sam Carter had a way of talking so quickly even Adele sometimes struggled to keep up. He had the manner and, in her assessment, appearance of a golden retriever, with dyed blond hair an inch past protocol, an upturned nose, and chocolate eyes.

Agent Carter reached across the seat and gripped John by the hand, before the French agent could even react. He began pumping John's hand up and down, genially, and in a chipper tone, declared, "Welcome to the States. Is it your first time?"

Adele winced, reading the lines pressed around John's cheeks and the glower in his eyes. "Thank you," he said, tight-lipped.

Carter shook John's hand a little bit longer. Adele had always known Agent Carter to be a friendly sort. She had appreciated it when she'd been at the agency. But she could tell, just by watching, that John was looking forward to wiping his hand off on the seat next to him and glaring at the back of their driver's head for the journey north to the crime scene.

"Well, buckle up, you guys!" Sam said, still cheerful, oblivious to Renee's glower.

Adele winced over the back seat at John, and he just glared at her. She half extended a hand as if to shake as well, and he tucked his hand deep in his pocket.

83

Adele could sympathize somewhat. In France, people didn't express their affection in the same way with complete strangers. There had been times in Paris where Adele had walked down a street without a single person nodding or waving at her. She supposed John would have to acclimate on this side of the pond.

The car took them away from the airport, along the stretch of highway, meandering through the traffic, and then heading north, toward where the body had been dumped.

Through the duration of the journey, Agent Carter tried to strike up a conversation, and while Adele answered his queries in short, single-syllable responses, John ignored him completely. Eventually, even the gregarious agent fell quiet. The sky was laden with clouds, and more swept in across the horizon. A gray tinge eventually fell over the highway, like a funeral procession heralding their approach. Adele shivered, leaning against the side of the car, her head resting against the cool glass as she endeavored to parse out what she knew about the case.

They reached the crime scene about thirty minutes later. By now, some of John's bad mood had rubbed off on Agent Carter. The happy-go-lucky young agent from San Francisco had lost some of the spark in his Labrador eyes, and he wasn't smiling anymore.

Which, coincidentally, meant John was.

The tall agent stretched his legs and stepped out of the vehicle onto the small, wooded path. Adele followed suit, and was immediately assailed by the scent of oak and stale sap. Pinpoint leaves scattered the ground, but sweeping crews had been by, dusting off the trail. The edges of the road were lined with large piles of these gathered leaves, and Adele spotted rustling and trembling detritus, suggesting a squirrel or chipmunk had found a safe haven amidst the dross.

She walked along a cracked asphalt road that seemed in poor use.

"Body's not here anymore," said Agent Carter, briskly, lest he entice John's ire again. He waved a hand toward the trees. "Couple of joggers found her. Bled dry."

Adele looked around and said, "This wasn't the scene where she was killed?"

Agent Carter shook his head. "Doesn't look like it. No blood spatter. She was dumped here."

Adele and John moved toward three orange traffic cones set up in a triangular shape which marked out where the body had been discovered in the center of the road. She nudged John and nodded.

"Think he just pushed her out of the back of a car?"

John scratched his chin. He replied in English, his accent thick. "Possibly. Could've come from the woods?"

Adele looked to the trees, and at the slope angle leading up to the trail. She pointed further down the path. "Would've dumped her there if from the woods. The trail on either side here is too steep. Would've made our killer's job a ton harder, lugging a body up this way." She hummed in thought and shook her head in finality. "No—I think he was in a car. Dumped her in the middle of the road now that he was done with her."

Adele and John moved along the trail a bit longer, but there was nothing much to find. The body had been taken to the morgue, and the report would be forthcoming. Beyond that, other vehicles had come through, ruining any potential chance at finding tire tracks.

Still, one could never be too careful. "We should photograph the road," she said to Agent Carter.

He nodded. "On it. Agent Grant suggested the same."

Adele smiled softly at the mention of her old boss. "This wine-making shop—Artisan's Supplies... how far is it?"

"Only two miles," he stammered.

"Take us."

A short trip later, John and Adele once again stepped out of the vehicle. Agent Carter also disembarked, and now, seemingly intent on earning Renee's trust, he was trying to be more helpful than before. This, Adele knew, would only irritate John further. But she decided to let it play out.

"Here, Agent Renee, I can help with the door."

"Stop," John grunted.

Agent Carter had to jerk his hand back before getting it slammed in the doorjamb. John looked at the younger agent. "Which one is the victim's car?"

Agent Carter looked delighted he had something to offer that John needed. "Here," he said, quickly, "look, just right here." He gestured toward a vehicle in the nearly empty lot.

A couple of other cars were tucked around beside the building, and Adele's eyes flicked up, noticing a white security camera facing the parking lot. She nudged John and pointed.

He nodded, but then approached the indicated vehicle—an old, white sedan.

"I was told she left a pile of supplies nearby," John said.

Agent Carter replied, "Already back at the lab. It was wine-making stuff—a glass carboy, and double-level corker. They're tagging and bagging, but they don't think the killer touched it. It looked like she bought it from the store, then dropped it. Clerk confirms the purchase."

John nodded once, and Agent Carter looked like he'd been awarded a medal. He began beaming again, and John's mood seemed to darken a little more. Adele rolled her eyes and began circling the car, her eyes flitting. Nothing of note. Just an old vehicle. The plates had already been run. Everything was legal. Not even a traffic ticket outstanding.

She looked back toward the store, her gaze darting to the camera again.

She stood for a moment, beneath the gray clouds still pulling across the sky. She breathed softly and closed her eyes. The woman had been taken here. Killed somewhere else, then dumped on a road two miles away. The person had done so quickly. They must have known the area and planned it out. Were they a local? They'd killed in Germany, then France, and now in California. How familiar were they with these places?

Adele shivered a bit and rubbed at her sleeves. She was in a new suit, thankfully, no longer boasting wrinkles from sleeping overnight in a motel room.

She glanced at John. "See anything in the car?"

He shook his head. "Nothing."

"Didn't think so. I'm going to talk to the clerk. You guys can keep flirting out here, or follow me." She glanced back up at the security camera for a moment, certain she glimpsed a small red light.

Maybe the eye in the sky had spotted something they'd missed.

She moved toward the wine-making shop and approached the sliding glass doors, onto a pink brick walkway. A couple of other stores flanked the wine shop on either side, and Adele took note before passing through the sliding doors into an air-conditioned room, in desperate hope the security camera had spotted *anything*.

CHAPTER SEVENTEEN

Artisan's Supplies was in a much better state than the facade of the building. The sign had shown peeling letters, and the pink bricks looked like they'd been red once upon a time. Inside, though, whoever owned the store kept the place immaculate.

Adele spotted various accoutrements lining the wall. Large, wooden barrels neatly arranged against the back wall, with small hooks attached to bungee cords holding the containers in place in such a way that would allow one to remove the lower containers in the stack without toppling the entire display.

Adele even detected a faint hint of pumpkin spice on the air, and she glanced toward the counter, listening to the quiet whistle of woodwick candles placed in an arrangement around a cash register half-hidden behind a row of pamphlets and magazines boasting subjects one might expect to find in such a store.

"Can I help you?" the clerk behind the counter asked.

The clerk had a thin torso, but large, round cheeks. She was smiling genially, but her eyes kept glancing between Adele, Agent Carter, and Agent Renee with flicking motions that almost seemed to match the soft sputter of the candles.

"I hope so," Adele said, displaying her credentials and then reaching the front of the counter. She absentmindedly poked at a dangling car-scent ornament—a foam tracing of red triangles in a plastic wrapper which boasted the ability to fill one's car with the scent of strawberry wine.

The clerk winced, scanning Adele and flicking her eyes over her rosy cheeks toward the two other agents. "Is this about the girl again?"

Adele nodded once. "What can you tell us?"

The clerk simply shook her head. "As I told the officers who came in a few hours ago—I remember her purchasing some supplies, saw her move out into the parking lot, but that's about it."

Adele stared at the clerk for a second. The woman was glancing off to the side every couple of words, though she seemed to be trying to fix her gaze on Adele. A nervous tic? A dishonest one?

"Is that all you saw?" Adele asked.

The clerk shrugged, muttered to herself, then sighed and crossed her arms over her crisp white uniform in a defensive posture. Her silver earrings caught the light cast by the candles, and she cleared her throat and said, "Look—I'm not one to pry. I did notice she dropped one of the items she'd purchased. A glass decanter by the looks of things. But I had other customers to attend to."

"She dropped it? As in someone assaulted her and she—"

"No, no certainly not!" the woman exclaimed. "I would have immediately called the police if I'd seen anything like that. No—rather, she seemed a bit overburdened with everything she purchased. Newer customers can be like that sometimes." She shrugged. "Two trips instead of one can save a world of headache." The clerk nodded sagely at her own advice.

Adele mirrored the gesture if only to further put the clerk at ease for what she asked next. Adele didn't doubt the woman's story. Perhaps the victim really had dropped her item by accident. Perhaps the killer had spotted this and taken advantage of a vulnerable situation.

Adele indicated the front glass panes and gestured with her fingers. "Any chance I could get a look at that security footage?"

The clerk chewed on her lip for a moment. She half glanced back across the store, as if looking for a manager or some form of permission. But then she sighed and said, "Can't see that it would hurt. Here, step around." She pushed open a small, swinging wooden door, allowing Adele entry behind the counter.

Agent Carter tried to follow, but John stepped in front, bumping past him and crowding the area behind the counter, forcing the younger agent from the San Francisco office to wait on the other side of the divide.

The clerk pulled open a drawer beneath the cash register and fiddled with a large black box, muttering and cursing a couple of times. Adele resisted the sudden urge to scream, clenching a fist to hold back her sudden rush of frustration. Finally, though, after what felt like a year, the woman pulled out an LED display screen, placed it next to the register, and muttered, "We only have the one. And it's as old as bones. But here it is."

After another few muttered expletives and some more fiddling, the clerk finally managed to project the image from the security footage onto the small display screen. Adele and John both leaned forward so

88

far their shoulders pressed against each other. The clerk gave a nervous little chuckle and then waited as the image played.

Adele witnessed extraordinarily grainy footage as a woman carrying a brown box walked into frame. She watched as the woman placed the box on the trunk of her car, and then accidentally dropped something out of the bottom.

A few seconds later, she witnessed someone just out of frame, talking to the woman.

Adele frowned. "Any way we can see who that is?" she asked, jabbing a finger.

The clerk winced and shook her head. "Only the one camera—sorry."

Adele sighed and returned her attention to the screen. The person out of frame didn't seem to have alarmed Ms. Wagner. She was smiling genially, even gratefully, nodding quickly and then pushing her box beneath the car.

Adele watched as she moved off with the person toward another vehicle.

"Hang on—there!" John said, sharply. "Can you rewind?"

The clerk's cheeks reddened a bit, and it seemed like she might be holding back a burst of frustration, but after another few moments of finagling, she managed to rewind to the portion John had wanted. "There, stop!" he said.

The woman sighed and did just that. John tapped a calloused trigger finger against the screen. "There," he said. "See?"

Adele did. The corner of a man's shoulder, the very edge of his neck. She watched as the man led the victim away toward another parked vehicle. This second vehicle was nearly entirely out of the camera's view—but Adele did notice two things.

"A white van," she said, quietly. "Too wide to be a sedan. Definitely white."

John nodded as well, confirming the observation.

They watched the tape through until the figures disappeared, then watched it again. At last, Adele looked up, addressing Agent Carter this time. "We need the office to run people in the area who own a white van."

"Could be a truck," John said, quickly. "Americans like trucks, yes?"

Adele snorted, but said, "If that's where he bled her out and

89

dumped her, it's more likely a van. A truck wouldn't suit his purposes."

John shrugged, stepping back through the swinging wooden door set behind the counter. "Could be a truck," he insisted.

They both turned now to Agent Carter, who was hesitating, looking at them with an expression caught somewhere between apologetic and worried. The second part of the emotion seemed mostly directed toward John. He winced as he said, "Actually, not sure we can do that. I already spoke to the office before you guys arrived. Was looking for some help tracking down recent arrivals from France."

Adele nodded once, impressed. "Good call," she said. "So why the long face?"

He winced at her again, seemingly glad to address Adele rather than her surly partner. "They're already checking passengers that flew from France to San Francisco in the time frame between your last murder and this one. Already an enormous undertaking, even given the resources we have." He shrugged. "I spent a good amount of time as an analyst and data engineer before moving into this position. I know how much leg work goes into it."

"You're saying they won't be able to look for a van? Can you ask?"

Carter just shook his head. "I'm saying there's no point in even asking. I know the lead on the data side of this case. She won't force anyone to work overtime—not this week. Scanning passengers that flew in from France is already wearing them thin."

Adele puffed her cheeks. "So the van is a no go?"

Agent Carter hesitated, but then clicked his fingers. "Well—not as a new search... But, if you're okay with it, they might be willing to attach it to the search they're already running. Could help narrow it down—finding out locals from France who own a van in the area."

John snorted and spoke, but his accent caused Carter to lean forward to hear better. "Might also completely miss our culprit. We don't know the van is his—nor do we know he's a local. Could be from France, or from Germany. What is it you Americans say—this is a... *pickle?*"

"Might not be from any of those countries," Adele replied. "Could be killing for fun in foreign nations."

John tapped his nose and pointed toward his partner. They both looked at Agent Carter, waiting. The young man winced and said, "It's worth a shot. I promise, they won't take on a separate search. Already they're trying to run hundreds of people in the next forty-eight hours. Best we can do is send them the van parameter, and help them narrow."

Adele sighed. "Could you at least ask?"

Agent Carter shrugged. "Sure—but I know what they'll say." He turned, pulling his phone from his pocket and moving toward the large glass windows.

Adele and John waited in silence, save the sputter from the woodwick candles. After a few moments, Carter turned, shrugging and shaking his head apologetically. "They'll add the van to their search," he said, "but aren't willing to conduct a new one. Not enough resources. Sorry."

Adele closed her eyes, inhaling the scent of pumpkin spice and fresh wood in the small shop. It wasn't ideal... but it would have to do.

If the killer *wasn't* from the area—it would be a huge waste of time. She could only hope he was a local... But if so, he knew this area, which meant catching him before he killed again might be an impossibility.

CHAPTER EIGHTEEN

Not all angels had wings, nor did their servants fly, yet Gabriel felt downright buoyant as he stood stark naked in his backyard, staring at the flames flickering up from the small stone pit in the center of the grass. He watched as his clothing burned. The cool air against his unclothed body sent chills and prickles across his exposed skin.

Gabriel looked to the sky, watching as gray clouds pulled close. Those who served Odin often were fond of gray. Those who thought of Zeus knew that clouds heralded destiny. Those who followed Ra thought it an ill omen, though.

Gabriel looked at the burning clothing in the fire pit. His hands were rubbed raw and stained—he could even smell the faint odor of cleaning chemicals which had rubbed into his skin. His eyes flicked along the side of his home, toward the empty spot outside the house. He'd spent nearly an hour scrubbing the van—removing every last drop of precious elixir. Now, the van was returned back to its owner, who remained none the wiser.

His garden pressed up against a forest—no eyes would be watching him. No one would see a thing. No one could know.

The smell of burnt cloth soon overtook the faint lingering scent of chemicals on his fingers. He'd covered his bases. Scrubbed the van, burned his clothes. Returned the van fresh, clean.

The cargo, of course, he'd kept. He glanced down at the small cooler at his feet. Three liters of elixir… Three liters was precious few. Would it be enough? The gray clouds above suggested so—even the heavens now wished to conceal his actions, hiding them from the witness of the sun.

The lands beyond called to him—he could practically hear them screaming his name, beckoning him home. The gray hairs would come, the wrinkles would stretch… *To die is gain…*

The elixir would prepare his body…

He could feel the craving arising in his chest. He turned, still stark naked, grabbed the cooler, and strode purposefully back toward the house. He punched in the security code, slid open the glass door, and moved into the basement, down the final set of stairs, into the studio.

He passed under a sputtering yellow bulb and frowned up at it. He would have to change the light soon enough—darkness was only for the deserving.

He came to a halt in front of the small wooden table set into the display case of wine bottles. His eyes scanned the display, searching. The woman had been forty-three according to the information he'd received. His eyes flicked from the white labels with sharpie numbers. Where was it... the right vintage...the right year—

There. Perfect.

He snatched the bottle from the case and uncorked it with his bare hand. Then he grabbed his mixing goblet, poured a respectable amount of wine, and swished it around. He retrieved the small cooler, confronted by the odor of bittersweet liquid on the air. He grabbed a one-liter bag, and, without bothering to take care, he ripped the top with his teeth.

He tasted iron and a coppery tint. He winced against the sudden bolt of hunger. His soul was weary—it needed to revitalize. He needed this.

Gabriel poured, with trembling fingers, the contents of the blood bag into the wine.

He whispered softly, a prayer, offering it to anyone who might be listening. Then, once the mixture was blended together, he tipped the glass and began to drink, slowly.

The trembling in his hand only grew worse. He gritted his teeth, growling against the liquid sloshing them.

"Preserve me," he muttered and grabbed a second bag from the cooler. As he did, his elbow knocked into the wine bottle on the table. It crashed to the stone floor, shattering, sending purple liquid spewing over the floor.

"Damn it!" he shouted. His hands still trembled. His soul was still weak. He could feel it, lurking in his stomach. The flesh could only be destroyed by the spirit! But his spirit was too weak—too weak to even fight!

He grabbed one of the blood bags, ignoring the wine now, and ripped it with his teeth, shoveling the elixir into his mouth, allowing it to run down his cheeks, splash against his nose. He swallowed, gargling, and then gasping.

The warm liquid spewed into his mouth but a second later, he hiccupped and... hesitating, feeling a wave of pressure rise to his throat, his eyes widened in fear.

His spirit rejected the elixir.

He threw up, doubling over and gasping at the ground, strings of blood and saliva and puke dangling from his lips toward the floor.

"Damn it!" he screamed at the floor. "Damn you—damn you!"

Slow.... he had to take it slow. Careful... The process of eternity couldn't be rushed... He knew this. Why was he acting like a fool? His spirit remained weak in him—his flesh was still strong. Too strong. It was forbidden to weaken himself naturally. Once, as a child, he'd tried to take his own life—pills and poison.

Swill. It would have killed his spirit as well. Luckily, he'd been fortunate. His spirit had survived. Now—his flesh was trying to control him once more. But he wouldn't allow it.

He dropped to his knees, retrieved the third and final bag, and then he retrieved a shard of glass from the base of the wine bottle. A few precious droplets of the wine remained. The mixture was important. Slow—careful. Strength came to the patient.

He exhaled, puffing his cheeks, still naked, leaning in a puddle of puke and blood and wine. It would all be over soon—it had to be. One way or another, this had to end.

CHAPTER NINETEEN

Adele and John moved across the parking lot back toward Agent Carter's unmarked vehicle. The air of dejection hung heavy as they left the wine-making shop behind them. The security footage had revealed barely a thing. They were grasping at straws.

Adele glanced sidelong at her tall partner. "How are you?" she asked.

He raised an eyebrow. "Fine. You?"

"Worried," she said. "The case... Robert's email—he's still not answering the phone..."

It was credit to how much John knew she cared for Agent Henry that he didn't say anything. Instead, he just looked at her, waiting.

The two of them reached the car and leaned against the hood, sitting on the cold metal and staring toward the shop where Agent Carter took down the clerk's information in case they needed to contact her off hours.

"What are we missing?" Adele murmured, softly.

"France," John replied.

She grinned. "Oh come on, it isn't so bad here."

John gave her *the eye*. His dark gaze fixated on her for a moment, his burn mark beneath his chin standing out in the lights from the shops against a backdrop of ever darkening skies. "You people smile too much. I don't trust it."

Adele nodded. "Frowning at everyone you don't know... Yes, much more trustworthy."

"Not frowning. Ignoring. The perfect solution to annoying strangers." John sighed in a forlorn, longing sort of way. "How I wish to be ignored again. Three people nodded at me as we left the airport."

"God forbid—they *greeted* you? How horrible."

John shook his head, rubbing at his nose. "You people are crazy."

Before they could get into it, though, Agent Carter burst from the small shop, waving his phone in the air, grinning wide.

John gave Adele a long look and jutted a thumb toward the exuberant young field agent. "See?" he muttered.

Adele rolled her eyes, but pushed off the car. "What is it?" she called.

Agent Carter reached them and, breathing heavy, he wiggled the phone toward her. "The office. Already got a hit."

Adele went cold, staring at Agent Carter. "Hang on—already? How? It's only been what... a half hour? Fifteen minutes?"

Agent Carter shook his head. "The van clue narrowed it down a bunch. I told you it would pay off!" He grinned at them.

"Even wild-goose chases can come back quickly," John muttered.

"Who is it?" Adele asked.

Carter breathed deeply, staring at the ground now, trying to gather himself. Adele waited, feeling impatience mounting. Finally, though, Carter looked up and said, "A doctor..." Another gasp. "And his wife." One more deep breath.

"Damn it, spit it out!" John snapped.

Carter winced and then, trying to speak without breathing, he rattled off, "They just returned from a European vacation. Went to Germany, took a train to France and flew home from there. Looks like they rented a van recently—sort of thing to haul furniture and the like!"

Carter desperately tried to recover his breath as John and Adele shared a quiet exchange.

"A doctor and his wife?" said John.

"Can't rule out a couple," Adele replied, quietly. "We've had a husband-wife team before."

John cursed, but nodded. He reached out and patted Carter on the back, a bit sheepishly as if feeling guilty for the agent's gasping. But then the sympathy faded with the gesture and he said, "How long ago did they get in?"

"Two—two," Carter breathed and nearly coughed, "two hours *before* the third murder. A tight window, yes... but possible."

"Good enough for me," Adele said. "Good job, Carter. Do you have an address?"

Agent Carter nodded, wiggling his phone again, then John growled. "Get in—I'll drive."

Adele winced at this. "You don't even have your license here," she began to protest, but John had already snatched the keys from Carter's extended hand and lodged his large form into the driver's side of the unmarked FBI sedan.

Muttering to herself about the number of ways they might get into an accident, Adele slid into the seat next to Agent Carter in the back.

"Oh, you sit in the back now?" John asked, putting them in reverse and squealing out of the parking lot.

"You know what a stop sign is, right?" she asked.

As if in answer, John blew right through the stop sign at the T-intersection which led back onto the main highway.

"Don't backseat drive," he called over his shoulder.

"Don't front-seat crash!" she retorted.

Her words were cut off by a buzzing GPS voice directing their vehicle toward their destination.

***

Destination is on your left... declared the GPS voice emanating from Carter's phone. John yanked the steering wheel—and, at this point, Adele felt certain he was playing it up for the sole pleasure of traumatizing his captive passengers.

The front wheels bumped over the curb and the sedan nearly hit a mailbox. Then John kicked open his door and Adele, gritting her teeth—without realizing she'd been doing it for the entire drive—kicked out the passenger door and joined her partner.

They faced a large, stone house with an octagonal turret in the front next to double wooden doors atop stone slab steps.

"Nice place," John muttered in French.

The house, for a brief moment, reminded Adele of Robert, but she repressed the rising murk of worry and focused on the home itself.

"Careful, calm," Adele muttered to her partner. "They're not guilty of anything yet."

"Ah," said John. "What you're saying is *don't* shoot the nice doctor and his wife?" He glanced back to where Carter had joined them, looking a bit sickly. "I'm joking," he said, for the benefit of the young agent.

Then the three of them moved toward the front of the mansion. The house was in the suburbs midway between Sonoma and San Francisco. Around them, the other homes matched this one—all large, all expensive. Just shy of *mansion* status in Adele's mind.

As they neared the front door, Adele held out a hand, pressing it against John's muscled chest. "Look," she said sharply.

First, she'd noticed the U-Haul parked outside the garage, attached as a trailer to a small mini-coupe. The juxtaposition would have been funny if not for the scene playing out through the large glass windows allowing them a glimpse into the living room.

Two people were seated at a long, glistening dining room table beneath a chandelier.

A man and a woman—older, but laughing and, in each of their hands, a glass.

"Is that wine?" John asked, slowly.

The doctor was older, but had dark hair. Possibly the man in the video, though it was hard to tell. The wife looked younger, and was one frame removed from movie star good looks. Still, she was the sort of woman who would have given Adele all sorts of jealousy back in high school.

John whistled beneath his breath. "Hello, darling," he muttered. "I like wine too."

"John, she's married, and possibly a serial killer."

John shook his head. "I don't judge." He moved up the stone drive, through the garden toward the front door.

Adele followed quickly behind, trying to match his long strides. They reached the massive oak doors, stepping past the windows. Adele reached out before John and tapped on the door. No answer. She waited, then extended a steady finger, pressing the buzzer.

A few seconds later, she heard voices—quiet, hushed. Then she spotted a silhouette through the glass, peering out into the drive.

"FBI," Adele called—though technically this wasn't true. Americans, though, had no clue what DGSI was. "Open up!"

The door opened without making a sound, but then stopped. A sliver of orange light, emanating from the dining room beyond, fell across the agents on the stoop. John's shadow was cast into the rose plants surrounding the house. A thin, olive-skinned face, with premature wrinkles around the eyes, and an overly large nose, stared out at them.

"Are you Dr. Gardner?" Adele asked, using the name Agent Carter had provided.

The man bobbed his head, his nose like a rudder, swishing as he tried to glance back over his shoulder toward the dining room.

Adele spotted a security chain, keeping the door half closed. "FBI," she repeated. "We'd like to ask you a few questions. Could you open the door?"

Dr. Gardner squeaked, and seemed caught between indecision. Again, he glanced over his shoulder. Now John was following his gaze, frowning. His hand had migrated toward his hip, hovering near his holster.

"Mr. Gardner," Adele said, quietly. "Is there a reason you won't let us in?"

He looked back at her and swallowed, muttering to himself a bit. Then he raised his voice, and in a deep, velvety, masculine tone, which, in Adele's assessment didn't suit his physicality at all, he said, "Let me see some credentials, please."

Adele hated to admit it, but part of her enjoyed seeing the doctor squirm. She didn't know Mr. Gardner at all. But she hated doctors. She hated hospitals. She hated anything that reminded her of illness or ailment, or death.

The last time she'd voluntarily gone into a hospital for anything besides her job had been when she was a teenager. Even physicals for the agency had been done through private clinics, rather than hospitals.

Adele and John removed their badges, and Agent Carter stood just a bit behind them, watching.

After the doctor looked at the credentials, Adele began to lower hers, but he wiggled his fingers. "I didn't see, one more moment."

Adele frowned, but held out her credentials a bit longer. The doctor wasn't quite looking at them, and instead, glanced over his shoulder again.

Now, Adele looked at John, and her partner raised his eyebrows.

"Sir, is there something you're hiding?"

The question seemed to alarm him. He turned back on her, sharply, and stared. "Hiding?" he stammered.

"Sir, I'm going to need you to get back from that door."

He let out another small squeak, which didn't match his normal speaking voice. "Look, it's all a misunderstanding. Just give me one second, and—"

"—No more seconds," John growled. "Open the door."

Adele wasn't quite certain of the legality of this. A fidgety, nervous doctor wasn't cause for entry. Agent Carter would have to report to his superiors. Then again, they were on the path of a killer.

With trembling fingers, the doctor unlatched the security chain and opened the door a bit more. "We're not hiding anything," he said, quickly.

"Sounds like you're hiding something," John retorted.

The doctor squeaked and stepped back as John stepped into the dining room.

"Hey," Agent Renee called out, suddenly, "stop!"

Adele followed his gaze, and she spotted the pretty wife, who'd also been sipping wine at the table, hurrying toward the top of the stairs curving past the dining room. By the looks of things, she had crept through the kitchen, around old, ornate furniture pieces stacked with potted plants, in order to reach the stairs without being seen from the door. Now, though, with John in the entry, she bolted, sprinting up the final steps to try to reach the top.

"Esther," the doctor cried, "be careful!"

John snarled, and bolted after her.

Adele stepped in quickly. "Dr. Gardner, let me see your hands."

The doctor stuck his hands in the air, protesting desperately and calling after his wife as Adele moved past, staring up the stairs. She heard John shouting, and the woman screaming. She heard the sound of clattering, which suggested they'd knocked over something in the hallway.

"John?" she called. "Are you all right?"

"We're sorry," Dr. Gardner was saying, shaking his head wildly, "it wasn't on purpose. We just thought, we didn't know—"

"Sir, I need you to be quiet." She turned her attention back toward the stairs, looking up at the dark outline of the hall. She could no longer see her partner, or Mrs. Gardner.

A few seconds later, John returned. In one hand, by the scruff of the neck, he had a small, hairless cat. In the other, by the collar, he had Mrs. Gardner. Frowning, he was leading both of them back down the stairs.

"Unhand my wife!" the doctor shouted.

"Happily," John growled back. "This is what you are trying to hide?" He wiggled the small, hairless cat.

"What is that?" Adele asked.

"A naked sphinx cat," the doctor said, his voice shaking. "Look, we didn't know that it was illegal to bring back. We wouldn't have bought it. There was a street vendor, they were very convincing, and I've never broken the law before in my life, neither has she, and please, it wasn't on purpose."

Adele stared. She looked at John, then back to Mr. Gardner.

100

"You're joking. You thought we were here for that stupid rat?"

Mrs. Gardner protested with a small little gasp. "It is a cat," she said.

John lowered his hand and said, "It looks like a rat."

Adele puffed a breath. "Mr. Gardner, I don't care that you smuggled in a cat. It's not my department. We're here about a murder."

Mr. Gardner looked shocked. His wife stared, and then both of them looked at the other, their eyes laden with unspoken words: *"What did you do?"*

The expressions were matching, the surprise palpable.

"Murder?" Mr. Gardner said, stammering. "We only just got back."

His wife nodded quickly. "What did he do?"

Mr. Gardner squeaked. "What did I do? What did *you* do?"

Adele breathed heavily, trying to calm herself. "You got back earlier this morning. Your flight landed two hours before someone died only half an hour from here."

The doctor stared. "Hang on," he said, quickly. "We got back only an hour ago. Our flight was delayed. You can check. It was. We didn't land till late."

Now John and Adele both turned, looking at Agent Carter.

Sam winced and said, "Er, it's possible. The search parameters were going off declared departure times from yesterday. There's a chance they were delayed. I can check."

Adele rubbed the bridge of her nose, glanced at the naked cat, at Mr. and Mrs. Gardner, then back at Agent Carter. "Yeah," she said, testily, "maybe you should do that."

Carter winced where he stood in front of the door on the stone slab steps. He was looking along the house for a moment, and said, his voice delicate, "That hauling van," he said, softly, "it's gray. Not white."

More good news. Adele stomped past Mr. Gardner, whose hands were still jutting toward the chandelier above the staircase. She approached Carter and looked toward the driveway. Her eyes settled on the vehicle in the drive. Indeed, it had been difficult to spot in the excitement, and the spectacle through the windows, but beneath the gray clouds, it was clear, the paint on the van wasn't white. It didn't match the video.

She sighed and looked at John. "Put the poodle down," she said.

101

"It's a cat," Mrs. Gardner objected.

John looked at the thing, like he'd found a booger, wiggled it a little, as if to see if it would move. The thing mewled, protesting the motion, and John gently extended the cat toward Mrs. Gardner. "It is very ugly," he said. And then said, "Have a good day."

He moved down the stairs, which split into two sections, and curled around the brown and white rail. He shrugged toward Mr. Gardner, and said, "You have a lovely home and a lovely wife. Have a good night."

The doctor just stared after John, as the man moved past Adele into the dark and toward the waiting car.

Agent Carter stammered a couple of times. "Don't you think, shouldn't we check the house—"

"Call to see if the flight was delayed," John retorted.

Agent Carter shook his head, holding his phone. "Don't need to. Just looked at the website. They're telling the truth. Flight was delayed, they did just get back."

Adele exhaled, feeling her breath tickle against her nose as it crept toward the chandelier. "So they're telling the truth. They couldn't have even been here at the time of the murder?"

"I guess not," Carter said. "Sorry. I didn't check. I just thought—"

"It's fine," Adele said, exhaling. "All right, we're sorry for disturbing you."

Mr. Gardner and Mrs. Gardner both just stared after them. Adele shook her head and moved back out into the dark, with Agent Carter falling into step. John had already positioned himself in the driving seat once more. He looked at her. "What now?"

She bit her lip, thinking of Foucault's demand for urgency on this case. Of Ms. Jayne's warning about the political implications behind the scenes of a tri-country, cross-continent murderer. "We do better," she said, simply, numb. "Or someone else dies. And at this rate, *soon.*"

102

CHAPTER TWENTY

They were back at a hotel, just outside of Sonoma County. Adele glanced sidelong at John, where he had turned from the reception desk, and began moving toward where she waited at the bottom of the stairs. He held a single key card in his hands, his thumb and forefinger pressed against it. He approached, and Adele began to roll her eyes, but then he shifted his fingers and spread the card, showing two.

"You have your own room this time, my lady," John said with a gallant flourish of the key card.

She would have been amused if she wasn't so frustrated.

John was normally the sort to take an elevator, but sometimes he allowed Adele's habits to rub off on him. She was in the mood for a good stretch of her legs. "What floor?" she said.

"Three," he replied, just as curtly.

The two of them began circling the stairs, one step at a time, their hands extended, braced against the railing. Adele could hear the quiet squeak of the varnished wood beneath her fingers. She didn't want to think too long about how many hands had groped these rails. She would make sure to wash her hands when she reached her room.

"What now?" John's voice came from behind, where he followed at her pace up the stairs. They reached the second floor landing, turned, and headed toward the third.

The halls were colored white and beige. A couple of hotel paintings hung from the walls. And flickering yellow lights set in torch stands lined the paintings. The air smelled a bit of chlorine, suggesting there was an indoor pool nearby.

"Now," she said, her voice faint in her own ears, "we sleep. Hopefully."

John cleared his throat. He continued after her up the final flight.

They reached the third-floor landing and pushed through the door, extending into the carpeted hall. A long red and blue carpet with white stars in the center stretched down from one side to the other. A row of mirrors lined the opposite wall, giving the illusion the hall was much wider than it first seemed.

Adele glanced at the room number on her key card, looked at the small little brown and white signs across from the open door, then turned left, following the silver arrow indicating her in the direction of her new room.

John followed as well. "Think he took a boat?" John asked, softly. "Maybe he flew into a different country, crossed the border through one of the checkpoints. That might explain why they're not showing up in a search."

Adele sighed, puffing a breath and allowing a lock of hair to rise and fall like dandelion fluff. "It's possible," she said, wearily. "Did Agent Carter say he'd be back in the morning?"

John shrugged. "Didn't really pay attention."

"Great. Well, I need some sleep. Whatever the case, the killer has been one step ahead. He knows too much. It's almost like he anticipated what we might do. He covered his tracks."

Adele came to a halt in front of her door, glancing at the key card, then at the brown number painted on the steel frame.

She looked at John. "This is me."

Renee waved with a wiggle of his fingers, and then moved toward the room at the far end of the hall, two doors down from Adele's. From the doorways between their rooms, Adele heard the quiet buzz of classical music. She glanced at her watch. It was nearly 9 PM. She hoped the music wouldn't last too long. She opened her door with the key card and stepped in, sealing herself in the hotel room and cutting her off from John's line of sight.

She tossed the card onto the small counter with greeting plaques and a small complimentary basket of soaps, then moved away from the desk, toward the single bed, and her eyes flicked to the TV. Whoever had last used the room had left the TV on a news channel. She didn't even want to look, and quickly grabbed the remote, turning off the device. Then, remembering the slick banister, she wrinkled her nose and hurried over toward the sink in the small bathroom. She lathered her hands with a fragrant soap that smelled a bit of honey, and then poured warm water into her palms, rubbing the soap clean, and with it, the feeling of germs.

She wished she could wipe her mind in a similar way. The killer was draining his victims, dropping them off in isolated locations. Three countries, and who knew if he'd stop.

Adele sighed, wiping her hands on a pink towel over the sink.

104

As she did, grazing her knuckles against the smooth, fluffy fabric, her phone began to buzz. She reached down, fishing her telephone out of her pocket; wiping her hand one more time to completely clear water droplets, she then clicked through with her other hand, swiping her password and holding the phone up.

Executive Foucault.

She winced, but then held the phone to her ear. "Sir?" she said, politely. Inwardly, she did some math, trying to figure out what time it was back in France.

The Executive's voice sounded strained, tired. "Agent Sharp?"

She huffed a breath. They weren't doing very well on the case. She figured Agent Grant back with the FBI was likely filling Foucault in on their movements. This didn't make her feel any more comfortable. She coughed delicately and glanced back at the small pink towel; her eyes traced to the caramel marble-patterned wall above the bathtub.

"Sir," she began, "we just got here. I know it doesn't look good. But really, if you just give us a couple of days, I'm sure—"

"Adele," said the Executive, his voice serious, "I'm not calling about the case. Do you have a moment?"

Adele shivered. It took her a second to realize he had called her by her first name. Foucault rarely did that. "Is everything okay?" she asked, hesitantly.

A long, huffing sigh. A pause, and in her mind's eye, Adele could practically see the Executive taking a long draw from a cigarette. Then another long, heavy breath. "I'm afraid everything isn't okay."

The tingle in her spine grew worse. "What is it?" she said, her voice hoarse. Before he spoke, her mind had already rushed to the worst eventualities.

"It's Robert," said Foucault. "Agent Henry. You are close with him, yes?"

Adele stared at the mirror over the sink. She could feel her breath—slow, shallow, as if she didn't want to breathe too loudly, lest she missed what he was saying. "Is he okay?" she said, her voice strangely calm in her own ears. It was as if she'd been expecting this, anticipating it. She had known the news would come. It was a resigned inevitability.

"No," Foucault said, simply. "He isn't. He's in the hospital."

"Is he alive?" Adele asked, and found her voice cracked halfway through the sentence. She wasn't even sure what the emotions were. It almost felt as if she were disengaged from her own body. And yet, she swallowed and tried the sentence again. "Is he alive?"

This time her voice didn't crack. Executive Foucault replied, "Yes. For now. He's in a bad way. I'm heading over myself. I don't know much."

"Can I call him?"

"I'm afraid not. He's unconscious. Not taking calls. I'll tell you what I can when I get a chance. I just know you two are close. I wanted to let you know."

"Should I come back?" she said, her voice trembling now.

The Executive's tone softened just a bit. And for a moment, his voice had the cadence of a father, a gentle, calming tone. "I wouldn't begrudge you if you needed some time. Agent Renee can solve this one."

Adele stood for a full moment, staring at herself in the bathroom mirror above the sink. She traced her eyes, baggy from too little sleep, down to her smooth chin, and back up toward her blonde hair. There were those who thought of her as pretty, in an exotic way. Robert had said she was beautiful with no reservation, the way a parent would. He had been there when her real parent had been cut into ribbons and left on the side of a park path. He had been there when she had wept, for nights on end, without relief. He had been there when she had first tried to solve the case. He had been there when she failed. And had been there when she'd failed again. He'd been an affectionate man. The father who had actually cared about her, rather than her career.

She felt hot tears begin to form in her eyes and reached up, furiously rubbing them away.

"Is there anything I can do?" she said, simply.

"I'm not sure. But I'm not looking for you to be a hero here, Adele. We have other agents. This case can be solved without you. If you need some time—"

"No," she said, without even fully realizing what she was saying. "I'm fine, it's going to be fine."

"Are you certain?"

"Yes. I'll get back as soon as possible. Solve the case, and come back. If he can call, the moment he wakes up, please—"

"I'll tell him. Adele, I don't mean to be crass, but if this is going to distract you, I need to take you off the case."

She bit her lip. She knew he had to say it. And yet she hated him for it. "Sir, I'm fine. Really."

This time, it seemed like Foucault was the one who needed to take a moment. Both of them waited in silence, and then, at last, the Executive said, "In that case, I'd be remiss if I didn't remind you the need for urgency on this case, Adele. Three weeks, three deaths, three countries—especially given the nature of the crimes. People are noticing. Political climates are tenuous already, we don't need further disruption."

Adele swallowed. She remembered Ms. Jayne saying something similar.

"I won't fail you, sir."

"Adele... In this case, just so we're clear, taking much longer *is* a failure. We need this one hushed before the media gets it. And if they do, we need to be able to say we already caught the bastard. Is that clear?"

"As crystal."

"Good night, Agent Sharp. Really, I'm sorry."

"Thank you, sir," she said.

And then she hung up. She didn't need that horrible moment to linger any longer. Sympathy wouldn't help Robert now. She couldn't help Robert. The urgency of the case pressed anew on her, but it was hard to focus on anything just now besides her old mentor. Victims on one side, Robert on another...

She couldn't help anyone. She stared into the mirror, her shoulders trembling. She placed her phone down on the small counter around the sink. Portions of it were still wet, as if it had been recently wiped down by cleaning services. She didn't care, though. She simply couldn't hold the phone.

She turned away from it, and then, looking back, dropped a towel on top of the device, covering the phone from sight.

Her hand, which she'd used to grab the towel, was trembling. She jammed the hand into her pocket and set her teeth, trying to breathe. She inhaled for five seconds, then exhaled for seven. A breathing exercise, in, out, in, out.

Her whole body felt like it wanted to shake. She felt like a tree caught in a tornado. Roots holding her deep, unable to move, unable to help, unable to do anything but weather the storm.

"Dammit," she said, growling. "Dammit, Robert. You selfish bastard..." She trailed off. She knew she didn't mean it. Why hadn't he told her? She had known something was wrong. Why didn't people tell her? Did they think she couldn't help? Did they really think so little of her?

You can't help, said a small voice in her mind. *You can't save him. You couldn't save your mother. They hide things because you're useless. You're helpless.*

She resisted the urge to scream. Part of her wanted to punch the mirror. She stood there, facing the bathroom above the sink, her hands clenched at her side. Then she just slumped, all fight draining from her like water from a sieve. What was the point? What was the point in any of it?

She unhooked her belt, placed her sidearm next to the phone on top of the towel. Not exactly protocol, but fuck protocol.

She moved over toward the door, and then shifted toward the bed, glancing up at the TV. She didn't want to go to sleep. She couldn't. She could still hear the faint blare of classical music coming from the room next door.

She felt caught, on fire, unable to do anything. Standing still was agony, moving was even more painful. Thinking. It all was a buzz—the fear and terror. Was Robert going to die? Would she be able to even see him again? She needed to solve this case. Politics be damned, but the sooner she solved it, the sooner she could go back and see her old mentor.

She could feel the tears again, spilling down her cheeks.

Was she really so useless? So helpless? Why did everyone have to die around her? Why couldn't she help? No amount of training, no amount of smarts, no amount of determination, no amount of practice, no amount of physical exertion, none of it seemed to stave off the inevitability that hounded every corner in her job. Death. Death lurked around every corner, and the hounds of Hades came for all. And all she could do was watch from the sidelines as one by one the people she adored were ripped from her hands. And eventually, she would follow. Death itself would come for her, nipping at her neck, cold fingers around her throat.

And perhaps it would be the truest mercy there ever was.

Perhaps death would be the answer.

These morbid thoughts swirled through her. She could feel the panic, she could feel the rage. And the despair drowned it all out in swishing, swaying tides of sadness.

108

She found her hand moving toward the door again, but what was the point? There was nowhere to go. Nowhere to run. Nowhere to hide.

She flipped the lights and lowered herself into a sitting position, her back against the door. Trembling. Shaking.

CHAPTER TWENTY ONE

And there she sat, for half an hour. Perhaps an hour, maybe more. Her pulse went wild, her heartbeat throbbing in her chest. A panic attack. Two. What was there to do about it? Nothing. Nothing but sit and wait. Inwardly, she loathed how she was feeling sorry for herself. This was about Robert. Not about her. This thought almost propelled her to her feet, but then another rush of pumping blood, a pulsing heart, and wild thoughts glued her to the wall, keeping her pressed to the floor, like a hand pushing down.

She offered up a quiet prayer, like her father used to teach. But this didn't seem to satisfy either. She tried to hum to herself, a song her mother used to sing. This didn't help. She tried her breathing exercises.

None of it seemed to stave off the dread pouring down her spine like ice water. A killer they couldn't catch. Her mother's killer had also eluded her. And now Robert, dying in a hospital, unable to talk to him on the other side of the planet.

A quiet knock echoed on her door.

She blinked in the darkness of the hotel room where she leaned against the wall. A shadow moved beneath the door, black lines crossing a yellow slit.

She tried to open her mouth to reply, but found she didn't even have the energy for that.

How fucking pathetic did she look now? What a joke. As good as a cadaver.

The hand knocked on the door again. The shadow shifted. "Adele?" said John's voice.

There was something about the way he said her name that carried a concern deeper than she felt for herself at that moment.

"Adele," he said, a bit louder, but still echoing with the same concern. "Open the door."

It wasn't an option. He wasn't asking.

"Adele, open the door, please."

Again, not a request. A strange tactic, she considered. Blunt, straightforward, a demand. But also full of concern, care.

She was just too tired for it.

"Adele, please, Foucault called me. I know about Robert. Please, just open the door."

She exhaled, her lungs compressing at the name of her old mentor. She reached up, her arm practically limp, and just barely pulled at the edge of the metal handle, twisting it, and allowing the door to click. It opened just a bit, jarring against her shoulder where she sat against the wall next to the doorjamb.

She felt John push the door and allowed herself to be scooted just a bit across the room. John stepped in, and his shadow stretched across her. She could hear the classical music again, echoing down the hall.

The door clicked shut. For a moment, she just sat on the ground, trembling, her hands wrapped around her knees, staring between her fingers at the carpet beneath her feet. Then John dropped to a knee. He wrapped his arm around her shoulders and gave her a hug. He felt warm in the cold room. He felt strong, his muscles pressed against her small shoulders.

"I think he's going to die," she said, softly, her voice trembling again.

He just hugged her again, holding her tight, leaning in and pressing his head down against hers, and then, whispering, his voice soft, in French, "It's going to be okay. It's going to be okay."

She knew he meant well. But his words irritated her. She half flinched, then turned, pushing away from him a bit. She shuffled back on her hands, her back now pressed against the doorjamb of the bathroom, facing the main entrance. "Didn't you hear me?" she said. "Robert is going to die."

John slid down the door now as well. He also sat on the carpet. He stared at her, his long arms draped over his knees.

"I heard, I'm so sorry."

She shook her head. "It's not going to be okay."

He returned her look. "Foucault thinks he's going to a better place…"

"That does fuck all for me right now."

John closed his eyes and nodded slowly. Adele glimpsed his scar beneath his chin, stretching and moving. The darkness of the room was near complete, save the moon moving through the open windows.

John looked at her in the dark. "I can't tell you anything helpful, Adele. I lost everyone I cared about. Helicopter crash. My fault." He

111

nodded and swallowed.

"Is that what happened?" Adele asked, grateful for the distraction. "Those pictures, back at the agency, in the basement."

He gave a ghost of a nod. "Friends. Brothers. I'd known them for ten years. Closer than any family I ever had. All of them, dead. I lost everyone. Nine of my closest friends. Because of me. I'm the only one that made it." He chuckled softly, but there was absolutely no humor in the sound, like the noise of a shovel digging a grave.

"Sorry," Adele said. She looked at John, looked at his scar. She'd known he'd come from pain, but hadn't known the extent. She'd known he was filled with guilt, but hadn't known the source.

He looked at her. "Yeah, well, I thought I was done. I thought that was it. Fast cars, guns, drink. I wasn't sure which would take me out, and I didn't much care. It was a little game; I'd make bets with myself, deciding if I'd live another year, a few months, a week. I didn't know. Then you came along," he said, his voice practically a growl.

Adele stared at him. He wasn't looking her in the eyes anymore. Shame and fear and frustration weighed on every feature. For a moment, she thought she could faintly smell the odor of alcohol. Perhaps he'd already raided the hotel fridge.

"I didn't like you at first," he said, stiffly. "You were too alive. Something about you wasn't right. Not normal. I didn't like you because I liked you. I didn't like anyone. Understand? I thought everyone I could like had died. I wanted them to stay dead. The way you smiled, it reminded me of one of my closest friends. Copilot. You have the same smile. Your cheeks half dimple, and your eyes squint just a bit. You finish it with a soft little sigh, like the start to a laugh."

To her astonishment, he was crying now. Adele wasn't sure what to do, or how to act. She found some of her self-pity was fading as she looked at her partner.

"For a while I hated you for that. But you reminded me. It was like someone had taken a knife to my chest and scraped away all the scar tissue, just to reveal the wounds again."

He shook his head, and for a moment, it sounded like he wanted to spit.

He stared at the carpet as well. "I don't know, I don't know, but I got to know you a bit better. I couldn't help but like you. You're hard not to like. You're determined. Focused. Unrelenting. You're a force of nature. A bloodhound. Made me think, maybe it wouldn't be the worst thing to live longer than a couple months. A year. Maybe it wouldn't be the worst thing to be sober sometimes."

He shook his head. "I know I'm an ass. I won't pretend I'm not. I know," he trailed off, "Christ. I don't know anything. But my point," he said, clearing his throat, nodding to himself, as if remembering there was a reason behind his words.

"My point," he said, "is that it's all right again. I didn't think it was going to be all right. But it is, again. Not for them. The dead are dust and the living survive. They no longer suffer, only we do. And it's all right. You still smile like him. My copilot, my brother, my best friend. You still remind me of my other brothers. You're determined, focused, brave. As brave as all of them. That's the highest compliment I could ever give anyone."

His voice strained again into a sob. His shoulders were shaking now, and he was crying.

Adele stared. She could feel her own tears slipping down the inside of her nose. She looked at the handsome, scarred agent. More scars than just the ones on his throat and chest. More scars than she could see.

She breathed softly, and for a moment, it almost seemed like she was inhaling his ache, his pain. Like she was taking a deep breath of the agony sitting across from her.

It's going to be okay, that's what he said.

But Robert was going to die. She felt certain. Foucault hadn't given much hope.

"I just want to talk to him again," she said, her voice shaky.

John nodded. "I get it," he said. "I'd give anything to be able to talk to my friends again."

Adele put a hand against the carpet and tried to rise, then thought better of it. She leaned over toward John and pressed her head against his shoulder. She moved up against him, the warmth of his body against her side. His muscular forearm against her trembling shoulder. She sighed softly, exhaling.

John whispered something in her ear, and she turned, looking up. He looked at the tip of her nose, and then his eyes moved to hers. He held her gaze in the darkness, illumination cast solely by the moon through the windows. The small shaft of orange light beneath the door pressed between their fingers, and between the small gap between them. The sound of warped classical music drifted through the wall

113

next to them.

"Adele," he said, softly.

She could feel the warmth of his breath against her cheeks. She tilted her head, angling her chin just a bit, looking him in the eyes and holding his gaze.

"John," she replied, just as softly.

He leaned in, and then put his lips to hers.

She held the kiss, drinking in the warmth, feeling the softness and the firmness, listening to the quiet, and then the pulse of a shuddering breath. Feeling the stillness of his body, and then the tremor of his heart in his chest.

And then she withdrew. She exhaled slowly.

He swallowed. "Sorry," he said, his voice faint.

But she shook her head, staring at his chin, not daring to meet his eyes. "Last time I tried to kiss you, you protected me from my own decision. I feel like I'm obliged to do the same."

"It's probably very wise of you," he said, in a husky voice.

"Downright responsible, that's me," she said.

"Wouldn't want to take advantage of me, not while I'm in this emotionally delicate state, yes?"

"That's right. Delicate—that's you."

"Adele?"

"John?"

And then he leaned in and kissed her. This time, it wasn't tentative or probing or hesitant. This time, he held her firmly, but tenderly, soft, but determined.

His eyes were closed, and her eyelids fluttered shut as well. He pressed against her, and she leaned back. Soon, she found she had moved, and now was leaning against him, one hand braced against the wooden door, the other pressed to him, against his neck, down to his side, pressed near his scars along his chest. She leaned into him, kissing him deeply, and then breathing softly. For that moment, in the sound of him breathing, in the shared warmth, the shared embrace, the shared connection, everything else felt faint, felt distant. Everything else felt like perhaps he was right, and maybe it would all actually be okay.

CHAPTER TWENTY TWO

The smashed bottle had come back to haunt him.

Gabriel stood, trembling, the final bag of blood still nearly full. But the wine was gone. He stared at the display rack behind his workbench. His fingers were trembling again. "Please," he said, desperately, "please, there has to be another. Let there be another."

But as he scanned the items, his eyes flitting from the labels, looking at the numbers, he realized the horrible truth.

That had been his last bottle from 1978. 1978, the same year the woman had been born; a crucial, important component of the task.

He looked longingly at the nearly full bag of blood dangling from his hand. His fingers were stained red and purple. He looked at the shattered glass, with dry glints of wine against the stained shards.

"Please," he said, desperately. "Please," he said, elongating the sound, his voice trembling now.

Desperately, he began searching through the display case, his eyes moving, flicking from one white label to the next. But he had organized perfectly. He knew what was there. And, before he'd even scanned the full shelf, he knew there wasn't another vintage from that year.

The blood in the bag was as good as useless; it wouldn't work. The age of the victim had to match the age of the vintage. He had always known this. Everyone knew it. Why wouldn't he think this through? How stupid could he be. How stupid!

He began to squeeze the bag of blood. His fingers punctured through the thin plastic, and the crimson material seeped down his knuckles to his palm, and then began to drip against the floor. A quiet tapping sound brought the droplets against the ground.

"Dammit," he murmured.

Of course, damnation was for others. His was a future of eternity. Paradise waited.

He looked into the mirror, just above the wine cabinet. And for a moment, he froze. He clenched the crushed blood bag in one hand. The dripping sound still emanated in the quiet basement. He leaned in now, careful not to step on the glass of the shattered bottle.

Was that a wrinkle?

His fingers pressed to his forehead. His hands combed through his hair. And he froze, his palm half pressed against his head. There, right beneath his pinky.

He leaned in, so close his nostrils fogged the glass, and he had to wipe hastily with his clean hand.

He dropped the blood bag from the other hand and heard it hit the ground, joining the glass and the blood in the discarded pile of refuse.

Gray hairs. A wrinkle on his forehead; gray hairs. It was working. He was aging. His body was being taken. His spirit would beat the flesh. His spirit had to be stronger now, strengthening. And eventually, eventually so strong it would destroy his flesh completely. And then, then he could be free. And then he would claim eternity. *To die is gain.*

It couldn't be faked. It couldn't be manufactured. And he could not be complicit. The ritual had to do it. The elixirs had to do it. He had tried to kill himself once. And that had nearly been the cardinal mistake. But, by the mercies of the powers that be, he had been given this new chance. Young, handsome. People had longed for him. Had looked on him with lechery in their eyes. He had known their secret desires, he had seen in the hearts and eyes of men and women alike.

They didn't know. They longed for the flesh. He had to put to death the flesh by the spirit. Only those who put to death the flesh could possibly inherit eternity. It was the same story. In the far east, 10,000 years ago, in the contemporary churches, the old synagogues, the old halls of the Vikings. Every story, they all knew the truth. The flesh would decay. The flesh was death.

He began to breathe heavily, his throat constricting.

"Please, look on me with favor."

Gabriel gritted his teeth. He didn't have enough of the vintage left to match the blood. He would need more.

His eyes flicked to the vintages on the counter in the storage space.

Some of them were too young. Far too young. He would not kill children. Their spirits were already stronger than their flesh. They just didn't know it. No, children had to be left. Which meant his eyes flicked toward the very bottom of the case. An old vintage. 1956. And 1958.

Only two within the parameters. The only two that wouldn't cause the death of a child.

He shook his head; where on earth would he get that vintage?

He would have to consult the list once more. Perhaps he would even have to update it. He still had access to that information. Then again, he didn't want his credentials to be flagged. Too many attempts, too much access to those files, given the current atmosphere, might be costly.

He stood, still naked, as naked as the day he was born. A gray hair on his head, a wrinkle on his forehead. The flesh dying, his spirit strengthening. But at his feet, the discarded blood bag, a puddle of crimson, the wine and smashed bottle.

There was still a distance to go yet. He hadn't arrived. But soon, very soon. It had to be soon. He knew it had to be.

Another name. He needed to find another name.

CHAPTER TWENTY THREE

Adele stood outside Artisan's Supplies at the T-intersection, scanning the road. She was glad, secretly, John wasn't with her. Things had only gone so far. Clothes stayed on, and dignity remained intact. But she remembered Executive Foucault's admonishment and his warning about the careers of those involved in office romances.

She shook her head, trying to dislodge the thought. John was a big boy, and he could take care of himself. She looked down at her phone. She scrolled through recent calls. Robert's number—four calls unanswered. He wasn't picking up. Foucault wasn't picking up either. She doubted this heralded good news. She needed to solve this thing so she could return and see him. Foucault's and Jayne's warnings weren't lost on her either... She was on a timer—barring some political incident, the killer was operating at a waspish pace. More bodies would drop if she didn't pick up tempo as well.

Her eyes scanned the trail, in the direction of where they had found the body. Two miles away. She looked back at Artisan's Supplies.

The killer had been in a hurry.

He had kidnapped the woman, and she had been found only a couple hours later. Drained. How much of a hurry though? Had he gone in a direct path?

She made a chopping motion with her hand, pointing straight toward the path at the edge of the intersection. That was the way he would've left. From this shop to the body. A straight line. She felt a shiver of anticipation at the prospect of movement through the trees and the soft, gently sloping terrain. Not quite her normal jog, but close enough.

She counted the houses as she went. Two miles of road. Two miles was a long space. She could've driven it, but that would have defeated the purpose. She was looking for something specific, though she wasn't sure what.

Security cameras, witnesses, old ladies who liked to sit on front porches. Anything that slipped the killer's attention.

The space between the houses was wide, the houses themselves not particularly large. It was as she passed the halfway point, continuing on, still marching up the street, sweating a bit, her suit rolled up at the sleeves, that she paused.

She spotted an old rope swing dangling from a large tree. An abandoned tire, split at the middle, rested against the tree. A couple of roots, like rolling waves calcified against the shore, protruded from the ground in the dirt. Grass abandoned the dust closest to the tree, likely from children playing around the roots, and scuffing up the earth. An old two-story house sat at the very top of a small hill, facing the road. She spotted a thick red mailbox shaped like a rooster. The aluminum bird stood out against the backdrop of dusty ground and withered grass.

A sprinkler system, in front of the porch, was spraying waves in angled patterns through the air, in palliative care for the grass closest to the house.

Adele saw glints near the door. She paused, fully stopping now, and turned to look.

She glanced up and down the street one way, then the other, and then crossed toward the rooster mailbox.

The glint grew more pronounced.

She felt a flicker of hope in her chest.

She picked up her pace, now striding up the driveway, moving over the tangled roots and past the swing from the oak tree. As she neared, she realized what it was.

One of those Ring doorbells. The sort that activated with motion and recorded whatever passed.

She felt a shiver of anticipation and hurriedly walked up the path, ducking beneath the spray of the sprinkler, then reached the porch.

Through the screen door, she saw a fudge-stained face as a four-year-old child looked out at her. The four-year-old was wearing overalls, with one of the straps hanging loose. He had brown streaks, likely from some sort of cookie batter, or maybe a Popsicle, dripping down his cheeks and staining his shoulder.

The child looked through the open screen door at Adele, then turned and began to scream.

Adele coughed slowly and crossed her arms. She waited patiently.

The sound of the screaming child faded as he raced into the house. His thumping footsteps were met by a shout. "Elijah, quiet!"

A few seconds later, a lady in a loose pink shirt emerged. Her hair was streaked with gray, and she stood slightly hunched. She had the

119

boy's hand gripped in hers, and though she was admonishing him sternly, she also held him tenderly. The boy, despite the words, didn't seem scared at all.

The old lady in the pink shirt limped over, still hunched. She peered at Adele through the screen.

"Are you with IRS?" she demanded, one of her eyes nearly half closed as if from some sort of allergy.

"No, ma'am, my name is Adele Sharp. I work with the FBI."

If she had thought the words would impress the lady, she would've thought wrong. The lady grunted. "Don't know anyone with the FBI. What do you want?"

Adele winced. She waved a hand toward the Ring doorbell. "I'm sorry, ma'am. I don't need to take up much of your time. But that bell, do you think it would be possible for me to look at the footage?"

The lady looked at the bell, then back at Adele. "FBI?"

Adele nodded.

"I don't rightly think the neighbors would like it much," the lady said. She held the child's sticky hand and gently tucked him away behind her leg, as if protecting him. "We're not really the sort that speak with feds."

Adele nodded. "I understand. I promise I'm not trying to get any of your neighbors in trouble. At least, I don't think so."

"Shoot me straight. What do you want?"

Adele hesitated. She knew it was against protocol to discuss much of the case, especially the details, with a civilian. But the woman, with her half sealed eye, and her slightly bent back, still had a searching look about her. She was studying Adele, and for a moment, Adele felt like if she tried to lie, the woman would see right through it.

"Apologies," Adele said. "Look, I'm searching for someone who has killed people. Three of them. One in Germany, another in France, and one nearby. Left the latest woman on the road. Drained her," Adele trailed off quickly, and glanced back toward the little boy.

The woman said, "He doesn't speak a lick. Slow. Sweet, but slow. Drained of what?"

Adele shrugged. "Blood," she said, simply.

"Some sort of pervert?"

Adele shook her head. "I don't know. Definitely some sort. They came from that wine-making shop nearby."

The woman wrinkled her nose. "Wine is of the devil."

Adele winced.

But then the lady's face cracked into a grin. "Just joking with you. I like Moscato. You seem like a nice sort. I'd invite you inside, but I've just been vacuuming. If you don't mind, just wait out front. Anything to drink?"

Adele stared; for a moment, as the lady smiled, she felt like she was about to cry. "No, thank you though," she said, a flash of gratitude flooding her. "You think it's okay if I—"

"I'll bring you the video. I have one of them online doohickeys. Shows the moving pictures and all that stuff."

Adele hesitated, and the woman laughed again. "Still joking. I know what a video is. Hang tight. I'll be right there."

The woman disappeared through a side door; Adele heard the muttered conversation between her and the boy. The woman said, "Head upstairs, and go wash yourself."

The boy replied, "What?"

"Elijah, head upstairs and go wash yourself."

The boy replied, "What?"

"Darn it, child, I don't have time. Go upstairs. Look, see, look what Grandma is doing with her hands. See that? You go do that upstairs."

"What."

But this last time, it didn't sound so much like a question, as an acknowledgment. A few seconds later, Adele saw the fudge-stained child racing through the house and scampering up the steps, moving away.

Adele hid a soft chuckle and waited patiently on the porch. A few moments later, the lady reappeared. In her hand, she had a small iPad. She held it up for Adele. In the other hand, she had two glasses of iced tea held by the lip—the ice clinked appetizingly against the glass and the cool, amber liquid.

"Take your time, dear. I'm still going to be cleaning inside. Holler if you need me. Don't run off with that thing; it's expensive."

Adele nodded quickly. "I won't, I promise."

"I believe you."

And then the lady, still limping, moved back in, her pink shirt fluttering as she exited the porch once more, leaving Adele with a glass of iced tea and the small iPad displaying the recordings from the Ring device.

Adele scrolled through the files and found the day in question. She went back to the start of the morning from the previous day, and then settled in, sipping on the iced tea, and playing the video at four times the pace. Her eyes remained fixed and anytime she felt the urge to blink she paused the video. It would take a while, but it was worth it. Soon, she felt certain, she would find something. The killer had to have taken a straight shot. A direct drive from the wine-making shop, to where he had dumped the body. It was the only possibility.

And so Adele waited, watching, her eyes fixed on the screen.

***

Afternoon arrived, witnessing Adele still sitting on the white bench, facing the rope swing dangling from the tree, and scrolling through the iPad.

The old woman popped her head out of the screen door for the second time in the last hour. She had a plate of cookies and extended them to Adele.

Adele looked at the chocolate chip cookies and winced. "Sorry, I shouldn't."

The woman looked downright offended. "You should; a skinny girl like you. Come on."

Adele chuckled, but then, with a gracious nod, accepted one of the cookies. She took a bite, and decided to never turn down cookies from old ladies ever again. It was the single most delicious thing she'd ever tasted. For a moment, she felt a strain of sadness. Adele thought with a pang what her own mother would have been like if she was allowed to reach a certain age. Would she have been able to make cookies this good?

Instead of retreating back into the house this time, the lady moved out onto the porch. The four-year-old boy who Adele had spotted from before was now peering through the window, just above them, sitting on the windowsill in the kitchen and watching her watch the iPad.

The bench creaked a bit, as the lady leaned down onto it and sat. Her pink shirt pressed against her, and she heaved a steady breath.

"Are you all right?" she said to Adele.

Adele looked over. "I'm fine, still looking. I found a few cars, but none of them fit our description."

The old lady nodded once. She had a glass of iced tea in her own

122

hand, and took a long sip.

"Don't you sort usually work in pairs?" she asked.

Adele, her eyes still glued to the iPad, felt a buzz in her head, the ache of staring at a screen so long, but still had the wherewithal to nod once. She saw no harm in maintaining decorum.

"Well, what did your partner do? He piss you off?"

Adele chuckled. "What makes you so sure it's a he?"

"Pretty girl like you? No other option."

Adele looked over, and then grinned. "Maybe. That's very kind of you. You're quite beautiful yourself."

The older woman laughed. Now shaking her head, and causing her iced tea to clink with the cubes against the glass. "Mighty heavens what a bald-faced compliment."

Adele continued to scan across the iPad.

"Mind if I give you a prayer?" the woman said.

Adele felt taken aback for a moment. She looked over. "A prayer?"

The woman shrugged. "Helps me when I'm trying to find things. Lost my keys the other day, I prayed, two minutes later, I found them. Lost Elijah last week, prayed, found him. He was beneath one of the orange trees out back, trying to smoosh flies into the fruit. Slow but sweet, like I said."

Adele stared, and laughed. "Well, can't see how it would hurt."

The old woman nodded once. She didn't close her eyes and she didn't bow her head. She instead looked across the road, toward the path. In a stern, serious voice, she said, "Good Lord, there is a pervert roaming around. I hope you help this pretty young lady catch them. Thank you and amen."

Adele took another sip from her iced tea, her eyes still scanning the image in front of her. She could feel the exhaustion from sitting in one place for so long doing the same thing. But it was too important to give up now.

"FBI you said?"

Adele nodded.

"Good for you."

"Thanks."

The woman took another long draft from her iced tea. She looked out toward the tree, down the path, her eyes flitting over the pulsing sprinkler.

Adele looked at her, then looked back. "Is Elijah yours?" she said.

123

She could still feel the eyes of the young boy in the window.

The older woman shook her head. "Well, he is mine. But wasn't. Was my daughter's. He's my grandson. But my daughter ran off and left him with me. Haven't heard from her since."

Adele winced. "I'm sorry."

The woman shrugged. "Well, not much you can do about things like that. Besides, probably better for Elijah. My husband will be home soon, too. He loves the boy. They both get along."

Adele smiled. "What's your husband's name?"

The woman hesitated, then wrinkled her nose. "I mean this in the politest way possible, but I do not trust federal agents. Not even pretty, nice ones like you. So for all intents and purposes, let's just say my husband's name is John Smith. And I am Jane Doe."

Adele chuckled. "John Smith and Jane Doe, and Elijah. Sounds like a perfect family."

And then the woman said, "Hey, you missed one."

Adele looked sharply back. She saw the very end of a vehicle moving out of screen. She stopped and spun the video back. She strained, staring close, and then watched.

She went stiff.

A white van flashed across the screen, moving from one end to the other.

She replayed the clip. Then again.

Jane Doe said, "Find something?"

Adele felt a prickle across her spine. She zoomed in on the van's license plate. A white van, and the license plate was visible. She read it again, again. Then pulled out her phone, taking a picture of the plate itself and texting it to John.

"Thank you so much," said Adele. "I really appreciate your time."

"Happy to help. Just don't bother the neighbors."

Adele nodded quickly. She gave a little wave toward Elijah, who was still sitting on the windowsill. She handed the iPad back to the woman and then hurried down the road, breaking into a jog and heading back toward where she'd parked the car.

Her phone began to ring. She picked it up, breathing heavy.

"Adele," said John's voice.

"You get that picture?" she replied.

"Got it. What is it?"

"Send it to Agent Carter. Get them to run those plates, and get us

124

an address real quick."

John breathed. "Is that the van?"

"Damn right it is. Come on, get it to Carter, and meet with me up at the wine-making shop. I'm about a ten-minute jog out."

"Hang on, did you say jog?"

"John, just hurry up. Meet me there."

Then the phone clicked, Adele stowed it, and broke into a run, down the dirt path, along the hilly trail, moving quickly, her hair brushing around her as she ran.

It was the same van, she was sure of it. The van, at the time, had a body in the back. The van the killer had used to kidnap the third victim.

"I've got you now," Adele muttered. She picked up the pace, hastening back toward the parked car.

CHAPTER TWENTY FOUR

"Come on, let me," John demanded.

"No," Adele said for the third time in as many minutes.

"You're too slow," he protested.

"And you'll kill us by crashing; just sit down and be quiet. I'm going as fast as I can." Adele hastened, driving quickly, following the GPS barking out from John's phone.

She looked sidelong at him. "You sure that's the right address?"

He glanced at his phone from the passenger seat and looked up, his eyes narrowed as he peered through the windshield. "Sure as shooting."

"Excuse me?"

He looked over and grinned at her. "It's an American expression I learned this morning."

"Dammit, John, focus. Is that the right address?"

He nodded at her. "If the plates you gave me are right, that's where the van is from."

"Rented?"

John tapped his fingers impatiently against the window. He muttered a few choice words as a semi-truck pulled out, merging in front of them. But then he looked back at her. "No, not rented. Owned. Young fellow."

"Does this fellow have a name?"

"Ken Davis," said John. "Lives about fifteen minutes from here."

"Right, well, that's the van."

"I believe you. Sure you don't want to switch?"

"John, shut up. I'm going as fast as I can."

Fifteen minutes more complaining, fifteen minutes more in which Adele felt like strangling her partner. Any thought of kissing him had faded, replaced by the urge to duct tape his mouth.

At last, though, she pulled to a stop, careful to avoid the curb and the mailbox. She gave a pointed look at John as she parked like a normal, decent human being outside the front of the house.

It was an old condo, split down the middle. The left side marked *A*, the right side *B*.

"Which one?" Adele demanded.

John looked at his phone. "B," he said, quickly.

John and Adele exited the sedan and moved up the sidewalk toward the condo. John went left, and Adele stayed on path with the main door. She watched as John sidestepped around a couple of trash cans, and then leaned on his tiptoes, peering through a window into the garage. He looked over his shoulder and called, "No van." He gave a grim shake of his head.

Adele's eyes moved from the driveway, which was empty, toward the red door set on the left side of the building.

She hesitated, looking toward the garage, then flicking her gaze to her partner.

"Maybe he's hiding it somewhere," she said.

John shrugged. "Maybe it was stolen."

Adele balked at the thought. If the van had been stolen, it would be as good as going back to square one. No, she had to hold out hope. She moved toward the red door and looked at the golden letter *B* emblazoned over the doorknocker. She reached up and tapped on the door.

She waited, listening. No sounds came from within. She looked back at John, who was sidestepping the garbage cans once more.

She knocked on the door again.

Still no answer. John shrugged at her. He moved over toward the garage, and began sliding his hands along beneath the door. He seemed to be looking for a purchase to pull. But the door was also sealed shut.

John emitted a string of curse words, then approached the front door as well. He scratched at his jaw, glanced toward the neighbor's door, and said, "Do you hear that noise? I could swear I heard screaming."

Adele winced. "I don't think we should just break the door, John."

Before they could reach a decision, though, there was the sound of squeaking tires. Both of them turned and looked towards the end of the street, and watched, their mouths unhinging as a white van circled down the road, turned up the cul-de-sac, and approached the very condo they were standing in front of. Adele and John blinked at each other as the van was parked in the drive.

The door closed with a thumping sound, and two feet emerged beneath the vehicle. Adele watched as the figure stepped around the front, and a young, skinny teenager began moving toward the condo

127

door, whistling to himself. He wore a black T-shirt, far too baggy, with a big white skeleton on the front. He had his pants too low, and his hair was buzzed close to his head. Still, his features were sharp, and would have been handsome if he'd spent even a second focused on looking presentable rather than tough. Instead, he failed at both.

John and Adele moved toward the young man, stepping over the sidewalk onto the driveway and blocking his path as he tried to reach his door. He pulled an earbud out of his ear and looked up, noticing them both for the first time. He blinked, and tried to take a step back. John didn't stop him, but followed, with a lengthy stride of his own.

"Are you Ken Davis?" John said, his accent heavy.

"What?" the boy said.

Adele stepped in, and in crisp English, said, "Are you Ken Davis?"

He wrinkled his nose, one earbud still dangling from his fingers. Adele could hear the sound of metal, and loud voices blaring from the device. "Yeah," he said, in a noncommittal sort of way, shrugging with one shoulder. "Who are you?"

Adele said, slowly, "Is that your van?"

At this point, the young man, who couldn't have been much older than nineteen, seemed to realize he was backed into a corner. Both metaphorically and literally. Now John was between Davis and his van, corralling him toward the garage door, if only to keep his back up against something solid.

The young man stopped moving, despite John encroaching on his personal space. He lowered the earbud from his other ear and draped it over his one extended finger. "It's my van, so what?"

Adele exhaled. "Your van is wanted in connection to a murder. It was spotted on Darby Road, about ten miles from here."

His eyes seemed to bug, and his chin wobbled a bit. "Hang on, what?"

John snorted. "Nice try. We know it was you."

Adele, though, wasn't so convinced. The guy couldn't have been much older than a teenager. Plus, she'd had Agent Carter check.

"You haven't left the country in months," she said.

The kid shrugged. "Have never left the country. That's not a crime."

Adele looked at him. "Your van was used in a murder. Who did you loan it to?"

At this, he went very silent. His eyes flicked from Adele to John, and then, in a squeaking voice, he said, "I want to speak to a lawyer."

Adele glared. "You loaned it to someone, didn't you? Who?"

He didn't reply. Adele moved past John, now, looking toward the van, glancing in through the windows.

"Hey," he retorted, "you can't do that. You need a warrant! I don't give permission."

He jutted out his chin, and his tone had an edge that resonated with the words, *So there!*

Adele nodded, looking back. "You're not wrong. I do need a warrant. It's a shame."

John looked at her, then looked at the boy. "A downright shame," he repeated. He then moved toward the back of the van. "You're not giving permission?" John said.

The boy shook his head firmly.

Agent Renee grunted. "That makes sense. I wouldn't either if I was guilty."

"I didn't kill anybody," the boy muttered. "Now, about that lawyer…"

John made a big show of stretching and yawning. Then, elbow extended, he slammed it straight through the window in the front of the van. Adele blinked, surprised, and the boy stared. He began to gasp and sputter like a landed fish, and John reached in, muttering, "Oops."

Adele spotted a stain of blood down the edge of her partner's elbow, but John didn't seem to even register it on his pain scale. He reached into the van and unlocked it from the inside, and then pulled open the side door.

"You can't do that," the young man shouted, protesting.

"Technically, true," Adele said. "But also, he's from France. Warrants are a strange concept."

John nodded, humming to himself and glancing around the interior. "Why does this whole place stink of ammonia?" he said.

Adele stepped a little closer to the van and winced. She caught a whiff of the pungent odor as well.

"I want to talk to a lawyer," said the kid, gritting his teeth.

John was now rummaging around the front seat, muttering to himself. "Whole place smells, Adele. Someone cleaned it out. Even if there's blood here, we're not going to be able to get a test."

Adele gritted her teeth. "See anything?" she said, ignoring the boy for now.

John was now leaning across the front seat, avoiding shards of glass. He sniffed a couple more times, and then one of his hands angled beneath the chair, and he began fishing around.

"It's empty," he said. "Cleaned out. Whoever this kid is working with—"

"I didn't do anything!" the boy protested, sounding panicked now.

John withdrew, but then went still.

His elbow was still bleeding, but as he raised his hand, there was a smear of blood across his finger. It was thick, congealed. Not fresh blood. Cold, somehow—it had gotten onto his finger while rummaging beneath the chair.

He held up his hand, showing it to Adele. "That ammonia didn't get everything," he said, significantly.

Adele immediately moved toward the boy, turning him sharply and pulling her handcuffs as she did. He tried to protest, but then John came over, and Ken Davis went still, shaking his head and muttering, "This is all a big mistake. It's all one big mistake."

"You can tell us downtown," Adele muttered. "Or you can tell us right here, who did you loan your van to? You haven't left the country. But someone did. That someone used your van."

He hesitated, then muttered, "A friend, just to move some stuff. But that's it. He lost the keys. Someone took them. We just got the van back. Whoever took them must've—"

"Shut up," Adele said. "Fine, don't tell us. We'll figure it out later."

Then she spun the kid around, his hands cuffed, and began pushing him back toward their waiting car.

CHAPTER TWENTY FIVE

It was a scene as familiar as a play she'd rehearsed. Adele sat across the table from their interrogation suspect. John leaned next to her. Agent Carter was taking notes beneath the single security camera above.

Adele shared a look with John, then fixed her gaze back on the small, thin, T-shirt-wearing kid. The black skull shirt didn't seem so tough anymore. He had a look like a frightened lamb, his eyes wide as they flicked from John to Adele.

"Who did you give your van to?" Adele said. It wasn't the first time she'd asked the question. And it wasn't the first time he dodged it.

"I want to speak to my lawyer," he said.

"Lawyer is coming," Adele said. "Wouldn't you rather tell us who you loaned that van to? You're young, what..." Adele said, glancing at the file beneath her elbow. She made a big show of looking through the envelope, even though she'd memorized the information already. "Only nineteen?" she said, giving a low whistle.

John looked at her. "Nineteen?" He winced. "A murderer at that age? You're not gonna survive in Gen-pop," he said.

The kid looked at John, and then back to Adele. "Seriously, I can't understand a single word he's saying."

John's expression darkened. Adele interjected before he could retort. "Look, kid, I get it. You're loyal. I can tell. Whoever you're backing for, I'm impressed. Really."

"All I wanted in the world was to impress you," the kid muttered.

Adele shook her head and looked at John; he shrugged back at her.

For nearly the last half hour, they'd been trying different tactics, but the kid wouldn't talk. He was tight-lipped, and seemed to be simply waiting for his lawyer. Already, they were stretching things as far as the law was concerned. Soon, they would have no choice but to step back and give the kid what he wanted.

Adele sighed, shaking her head. "You know what, I have to say, I do admire your loyalty," she said. "Look, we both know you didn't do this. You couldn't have. You never left the country. But whatever; I figure the best I can do is to let you think about it a bit. Can you at least do that?"

He looked warily at her, clearly noting the sudden change in her mood. Still, he seemed glad they were no longer yelling at him, and he hesitantly nodded once. "I can think."

"Good," Adele said, before John could lunge at the low-hanging fruit and make some obnoxious comment. "I'm glad. I know you're being loyal, and I respect it, but there are lives on the line."

He shrugged, but didn't reply.

Adele made a big show of sighing. "You know what, I appreciate your time. And honestly, I'm sorry about your car. We didn't mean to break your window."

The kid rolled his eyes, but didn't say anything.

Adele said, "I'd like to give you a phone call. Just to make it up to you. You can call anyone; your lawyer will be here soon as it is."

The kid hesitated, and his eyes narrowed for a moment. He glanced from Adele to John, but then said, "Where are you taking me to make that call?"

Adele held up her hands. "Nowhere, no tricks. We'll leave, and we'll bring the phone in here for you."

The kid looked up at the camera. "You have to turn that off too."

Adele made a small crossing motion over her heart. "The light will stop blinking, and you'll know it's done."

The kid crossed his arms now and leaned back. His hands were still cuffed, and the loose chain rattled beneath his wrists as he shifted. Adele gestured at John and Agent Carter. The two of them got up and left the small interrogation room, following Adele out into the hall.

She pointed at Carter and said, "Get him that phone, please. And turn off the camera."

Agent Carter winced. "I'm not sure if—"

"Just do it," John snapped. "Be useful for once."

Agent Carter looked hurt, but didn't protest anymore. Over the last few hours, Carter seemed to have grown more and more frightened by the tactics the two agents were employing. But Adele didn't care. Right now, she needed to catch a killer before he murdered someone else.

As Carter hurried off to fetch the phone and set up the call, Adele looked at John.

"Think it'll work?" John said.

"Probably. He's covering hard for someone. You only do that for

132

family."

"Think he'll call whoever he's covering for? What if he's involved?"

Adele shook her head. "He's involved, but not in any way that ties into the bodies. I think he's just covering for someone he cares about. He's only nineteen."

John shrugged. "I killed someone at eighteen."

Adele breathed heavily. "Well, let's hope he's not much like you then."

***

Adele watched through the opaque glass as Agent Carter waited patiently for the boy to stop talking, hang up, then wave through the window. Carter stepped into the room then and retrieved the phone.

The boy looked back up toward the camera; the red light had stopped blinking. He regarded the glass window behind him, but couldn't see through.

Agent Carter thanked the teenager and then left. As he passed, a man with a briefcase in a suit came the other way.

"Is my client in there? Mr. Davis?"

A brief exchange ensued, and the lawyer was allowed into the room with Ken Davis. Adele waited patiently, and watched as Agent Carter moved over, carrying the phone.

The moment he reached her side, Adele took the phone and quickly scrolled to recent calls. She held up the number and pointed it at John. "That's not the lawyer's number."

John wrinkled his nose. "Is that local?"

Adele nodded. She looked at Carter. "I need you to track this. Can you get that to me?"

Carter shivered a bit, but then said, "Yeah, shouldn't be a problem. You don't think maybe we should check with Agent Grant to make sure—"

"Carter, we're handling this case. How about you just let us take the flak, and you do as I say?"

The young agent shrugged and then took the phone from Adele, looking at the number, and moved off, putting his own cell to his ear and relaying the information through the device. Adele and John waited impatiently, arms crossed, glancing between each other, and then back toward where Sam Carter spoke on the phone.

The address associated with a phone number would not take long at all.

Adele glanced at her watch, and then back through the glass where the lawyer was talking with the teenager. Davis was gesturing toward the window and muttering something.

The lawyer looked outraged. Adele didn't really care. There was a chance they might get in trouble for some of the tactics. Bashing his window hadn't been exactly kosher detective work. But right now, she wanted to catch a killer. It would be up to the lawyers to figure how to keep him from killing.

Adele waited another few moments, and then Agent Carter moved back toward her.

"Well?" she said.

Carter pointed to John. "It *is* local. Kid's uncle."

Adele shared a significant look with her partner. "See, family. And this uncle, has he recently been out of the country?"

Agent Carter was nodding. "Yeah. Actually, his job makes it so he has to a lot."

Adele stared. "What's his job?"

Carter glanced back at his phone, as if to jog his memory. He blinked. "Did you get the file yet?" They should be sending it."

Adele looked at her own phone and shook her head. John looked at his, and then, both their phones buzzed. Adele glanced down and saw an attachment from an unknown caller, with no ID. She pressed it, dragged it to her phone, and opened the item.

Instantly, she saw a picture. For a moment, she thought it was a portrait of a doctor. There was a neat, clinical look about him. He was quite handsome, and was smiling, teeth dazzling in the camera. Next to him, she saw his information.

She scanned the info, then said, "He works for Lumen Relief?"

John wrinkled his nose. "What's that?"

She replied, "Like Red Cross. Pretty big. They do blood donations and the like."

John looked at her now, his eyebrows rising. "Blood donations?" he said, a significant tilt to his voice.

Adele nodded. "Exactly."

She looked back at Agent Carter. "This fellow," she said, glancing back at the screen and reading his name, "Jonathan Davis—he would have the perfect excuse to travel the world, collecting blood. Maybe that's how he finds his victims." She felt a sudden flurry of thoughts, and a slow prickle along her back. "Maybe that's why he's hunting them," she said, hesitantly. "He knows their blood type—could you look in on that? That might be how he's getting names."

"We don't know that," John said. But he stared at her, unblinking, his voice strained with concealed excitement.

Adele shook her head, her cheeks warm all of a sudden from sheer anticipation. "No, but it's a good guess. Right now we need to figure out where Mr. Davis is. We have an address? The phone number is local."

Agent Carter was nodding, grinning widely, his blond-dyed hair bobbing with the motion. "Yeah, should be at the bottom of your file. I can get the car if you want; I don't mind driving!"

"You wait here," John said, cutting him off. "I'll drive."

"Damn it—just get in the car!" Adele said, already moving, her fists clenched at her side. This was it. It had to be.

They'd found him.

CHAPTER TWENTY SIX

Gabriel stood in the bushes outside the two-story house at the top of the hill. His back pressed into the rigid bark as he leaned and inhaled the odor of oak and sap. Next to him, a small swing dangled, swaying in the late afternoon breeze. He inched forward, edging his nose around the trunk and peering up at the orange glow emanating from the open windows.

He spotted figures moving about the house. A family? Not ideal—but would have to do in a pinch. He doubled-checked the information he'd gotten from work, his eyes flicking down to the folded binder paper in his hand. With a trembling finger, he untucked the corners of the parchment and stared, scanning the note.

He had the right address. He glanced back up to the house, his eyes curving over the hill. The husband was his target. The next code year. The final vintage. According to Gabriel's notes, the man had ordered a case of Peach Moscato not long ago. A tentative connection—but crucial that the mortal and divine collide. Wine was crucial, and while this new victim wasn't directly involved in the making of it, he still consumed it enough. His blood would be properly tended, then.

Gabriel reached up, delicately brushing at his bangs as if coaxing in a budding plant. The gray had come—he should have trusted it would. His forehead had wrinkled, and soon... soon the aging would set in. Soon, he would be propelled onward.

He sighed, exhaling a deep gusting breath at the thought of this all finally being over.

And then his phone buzzed.

Gabriel cursed and snatched his phone from his pocket, lifting it and eyeing the number. He'd intended to hang up, but then he spotted the name.

His nephew—his late sister's son.

He hesitated and then answered the call. "Yes?" he said, in a curt whisper. He leaned back, hiding his silhouette behind the tree once more, no longer visible from the house.

"Uncle Jon?" said Ken's voice.

"What?" he replied, still curt.

"Where you at?" It sounded like his nephew was licking his lips. His tone, the question—it sent a prickle along Gabriel's neck.

"Are you all right?" he asked, closing his eyes now to listen close.

His nephew swallowed again, clearing his throat. Then he spoke in a way that caused the speakers to fill with static, as if he were cupping his hand over the speaker and whispering fiercely.

"What did you do with my van?" he said. "Cops came by—dragged me off. Said you killed someone."

Gabriel felt the slow prickle of panic creep along his back, but then sighed, swallowing back the fear, allowing it to coax him into the realm of inevitability. He'd always known it was a chance—a likelihood.

"The van? Used it to drop off furniture—like I told you. Cops, you say?"

"Yeah," another hiss. "I'm at the station right now."

Gabriel wet his lips but kept his tone neutral. "You tell them anything?"

"Nah, course not. You didn't kill anyone, did you?"

Gabriel sighed. "No—you know me, Ken. I couldn't do something like that. Look, hang tight. I'll figure out how to post bail. We'll sort this out soon. Just... just don't say anything, all right?"

"Fine... Yeah—fine... They seemed really certain that—"

"The pigs are lying!" Gabriel gritted his teeth. "You know they're liars, right?"

"Right... Of course. Sorry. I just... Never mind."

"Stay strong," Gabriel said, breathing heavily into the speaker. And then he hung up. He glanced back up at the house and then moved away, heading back toward where he'd parked his vehicle. He would have to plan quickly. He didn't have time to stalk, to track, to plan. Not this time. This time, he needed one last hit. That would sustain him—that would be enough. It had to be. It would set his soul free...

And if not... A cop's bullet could do the same. But first he preferred the elixir.

As for his nephew... Sometimes sacrifices had to be made.

CHAPTER TWENTY SEVEN

Doors slammed on multiple cars as the Adele and John led a procession of boys and girls in blue trampling across the front yard of a quaint, two-story home in the heart of Sonoma Valley.

"This it?" Adele shouted over to Carter.

The young FBI agent called out, "This is Mr. Davis's address!"

Adele pointed at two officers and commanded, "Check the back! The rest of you, follow me... Or, I guess, follow *him*."

She'd been in the middle of taking the lead up the asphalt and concrete driveway, when John burst ahead of her, thundering toward the door. He carried a breaching ram on his lonesome and rushed to the metal and wood barrier in the threshold of the house.

"Clear!" he called. "Mr. Davis, FBI—open up!"

No response.

John didn't hesitate. As the other officers swarmed in behind him, following after his loping gait, accompanying Adele as well, he swung the breaching ram and slammed it into the middle of the door. A loud crack accompanied a faint buzzing sound.

"That's the alarm," someone called. "We already informed the company."

John didn't seem to care—he was already in mid-swing a second time. Another crunch, then a crack and then John kicked out with a heavy boot and the door splintered off its hinges and toppled into the house.

Red brick with black roofing; Adele studied the windows—all of them covered. She felt a faint prickle as she marched up the porch and followed the other officers and Agent Renee into their suspect's home.

"FBI!" came a chorus of voices.

"Jonathan Davis—declare yourself! Hands up! Hands up!"

But though they spread out, weapons raised, scanning the area, there was no sign of Mr. Davis. Adele watched as three uniforms hurried up the stairs at the back of the wide hall. Above the hall, she spotted a single ornamentation of copper grapes. Next to a basement door, she noted a series of strange symbols and numbers. She frowned for a moment, and pointed toward the chalk etching on the brown wall.

"What do you think that is?" she said, moving over to where John's hulking form was framed in the hallway. He followed her indicating finger and just shrugged.

"Something abnormal, most likely."

"Clear!" came voices from upstairs. "Clear!" came the ones from the kitchen. "Clear!" came the ones from the backyard and the garage.

Adele clenched her fist. "Doesn't look like our friend is home," she murmured. "After you," she said, gesturing toward the basement door.

John opened the door, revealing a stone stairwell that curved at the far end, dropping off out of sight into the belly of the house.

The steps felt firm and unyielding as Adele marched with John down the stairs. Above them, she spotted two etchings of stars in the same chalk she'd seen upstairs. She noted them, but didn't comment, keeping quiet as John led the way with his weapon drawn.

They stepped into the basement, and after a cursory scan of the small area, John slowly stowed his gun, glanced over his shoulder, and called up the stairs, "Clear!"

As for Adele, she was already moving toward the strange assortment she'd spotted.

"This is definitely our guy," she muttered, bending over and scanning the wine rack at the back of the room. Glass from a smashed bottle scattered the ground beneath a wooden table, and an IV bag, stained with dried blood, had been discarded in the shadows of the table as well.

"Looks like our killer was in a hurry," Adele said, glancing at John. "Think Mr. Davis is out on another prowl?"

John just shook his head, moving over to study the find with his partner. He scanned the crisscrossing wooden wine rack and took in the glint off the mirror divider above the display case. He moved over to a bookshelf and began scanning the tomes on display, then let out a little whistle.

"Huh," he said, "look at this."

Adele got to her feet, moving away from the smashed bottle and discarded blood bag. She approached Agent Renee and also scanned the bookshelf. Instead of books, though, the case itself was scrawled with text against the back wooden partition. Again the scrawl was in white chalk, but this time it read things like, *"Spirit puts the flesh to death."*

139

And, *"Remember the code of Gabriel."* And below that, *"Don't forget payment for crossing over."* And another line that simply read, *"Stop saying, 'damn.'"*

John stared, shaking his head. "Guy's insane." He looked at Adele. "He's insane, right?"

She sighed and gave a shrug. "As much as any person who murders others." She turned away from the bookcase, now scanning the smashed bottle and discarded blood bag. "If he's not here," she said, trailing off.

"Think he's on a hunt?" John asked. "Or, I mean, looking for more *spirit*?" he said, reading the bookcase again.

Adele didn't reply, her eyes narrowed as she looked toward the display case. It was nearly empty. A few vintages at the top were from the last ten years. But these, it seemed, had been mostly undisturbed and some were even coated with a thin layer of dust as if they hadn't been handled in all the time they'd been down here. But then her gaze was attracted by two bottles at the very base of the wine rack.

"John, look here," she said, suddenly.

Adele bent and leaned in, eyeing the bottles and murmuring to herself as she read the labels. "See these? They're marked. Numbers."

John left the bookcase and, though he remained standing, he read the labels. Adele envied a sharpshooter's eyesight, but waited for him to say, "Numbers... This one," he said, nudging at the shattered bottle on the ground. "See... number on the base as well."

Adele pulled a pen from her pocket and, delicately, so as to not contaminate evidence, she tilted the edge of the smashed base. A white label with a number on it read 1978.

She looked up sharply at the wine rack. An identical label with a handwritten number also displayed beneath one of the empty compartments on the rack.

"Matches," she said, pointing with her pen and remaining crouched, her elbows pressed against her knees.

"What's the significance?" John said, slowly.

Adele scanned the rest of the case, noting more numbers. At the top, the numbers started with two and zero, and toward the very bottom, they were ones and nines. "John," Adele said, hesitantly, her gaze skipping to the blood bag. "What was the birth year of our third victim?"

"Birth year? Dunno."

140

"Check."

Adele kept her eyes fixed on the blood bag and the shattered bottle, as if fearful they might flee without her attention. A few moments later, as John scrolled through his phone, he said, sharply, "1978. Same as the labels. She was born in 1978."

Adele huffed a breath. "Thought so," she murmured. She reached out with her pen, tapping the wooden display case. "The numbers are years of the vintage... But... But I think he's matching the blood year—the year of his victim—with the year of the wine."

The moment she said it, she realized how it sounded. She looked up at John and met his expression of disgust. She winced apologetically.

"Gross," he said.

She didn't disagree. She pointed toward the top of the case. "Looks like he had some younger vintages—but they're untouched. Think he has a thing about killing kids?"

John's voice took on a growling tone. "For his sake, I hope so."

"Then that means he's after one of these." She extended her arm, moving the pen now and tapping it against the two remaining bottles at the very bottom of the wine rack. The pen against the glass made a dull *tapping* sound and she read both the labels. "1956 or 1958," she said. "That's the birth year of his next victim. It has to be."

"Older victims this time, then," said John. "The bastard is going after someone's grandmother, yes?"

Adele shivered, rising again and standing in the basement, detecting a faint coppery and fruity odor on the air that made her stomach churn. As she breathed in the basement air, she also faintly smelled puke. "Let's go upstairs," she said. "I'll get Carter to bag and tag and photograph. I need fresh air."

As the two agents turned and moved slowly back toward the steps, Adele murmured beneath her breath. "We know his motive, his name, his license plate and his address. We know his MO... we just need to find out where he is."

John led onto the stairs, taking them three at a time with his lengthy strides. "Think he's killing right now?"

Adele winced at the thought. "Let's check with Carter about blood type. It's the only connection I can think of—might help us narrow his targets."

They reached the top of the stairs and it took the agents a few moments in the chaos of the raided house to move through a sea of blue to find Carter. Eventually, they did, locating him against a backdrop of flashing lights and ominous dark vehicles with tinted windows blockading the road outside the house. Adele spotted a couple of pedestrians walking their dogs being ushered away from watching by two officers.

She noted other homes, across the street had lights emanating from their windows and citizens standing, peering out into the dark. The killer had been operating in secrecy—that, now, was no longer an option. But if they didn't find him soon, another victim might lose their life.

Agent Carter spotted them and at a wave from John, he approached like a Labrador, half-smiling and moving with urgent motions.

"Sam," Adele said, quickly, "my tip about the blood type. Have we heard back on that yet?"

Agent Carter winced and said, "I—I totally forgot. I was supposed to call them back. Sorry, really, just with all the craziness, I thought—"

"Sam," Adele said, impatiently. "It's fine. Could you call them now? How late is the lab open?"

Sam, though, was already fishing his phone from his pocket, nodding quickly and then scrolling through his contacts. He half-turned in the universal gesture of phone etiquette and held the device to his ear as he peered across the flashing police vehicles beneath the darkening sky.

A few moments passed, and then Adele heard a quiet, clipped voice on the other end.

"Hey, Amy," Agent Carter said, quickly, "look… No, no—it's not about that." His cheeks went red. "I'm calling about a case," he muttered. Then, his eyes shifting to John and back, and shielding his phone with a shoulder again, he muttered, "Fine—I had a good time too. We'll talk tomorrow, okay. I'm calling about the blood type. Is that in yet?"

Another pause, and Agent Carter nodded quickly. "Thanks—yeah, thanks. I'm with them now. I'll tell them. Great job."

He clicked the phone and looked up, his cheeks still tinged red. He glanced from Adele to John and said, in a clipped tone, "You were right, Agent Sharp. The blood types are a match. All of them are AB negative. From the victims in Germany, France, and also here."

"AB negative," said Adele, her eyebrows flinching at a sudden pulse of excitement. "Let me guess; that's rare."

Agent Carter dipped his head quickly. "Sounded like it. But another thing—all of the people were donors."

Adele was already turning though, looking at John. "We need to bring Agent Grant in on this. Carter, follow us!" Then she began moving back toward her parked car, her hand slipping into her pocket to pull her own phone. Gravel crunched beneath her feet and skittered onto lawn grass as she moved past the rows of cops.

"We need to look for donors in the same area, Sam. John... those numbers—the two at the bottom. What were they?"

Agent Renee rattled off, "1956 and 1958."

"Good." She reached their parked car and turned fully to Carter now. "I don't care if it is off-hours or not. I need your people to run a search."

Carter hesitated. "Like I said... it's office politics and all, but the lead for this week won't do any more off-hours. It's this whole thing from last month—fourteen-hour days and—"

"Carter, I don't care!" Adele said, shouting at him now. A couple of the officers nearby glanced over, watching them. Adele didn't bother to lower her voice. "Someone's going to die, probably tonight if you don't get this done."

Carter hesitated. "Normally... Normally they would—it's like I said, though. The data team has been refusing—"

Adele rubbed at her temples. "Fine—you do it then. Can you do that?"

Carter winced. "I'll need to go back to the office."

"That's all right. I'll put you in contact with Lumen Relief. Ms. Jayne, she's with Interpol, will most likely be able to make the connection, seeing as they operate in Europe too. You'll need to coordinate with them."

"And... all right," Carter said, swallowing and trying to keep up. "What exactly am I looking for?"

Adele exhaled, nodding, closing her eyes to focus. "I need you to find anyone born in the years 1956 through 1958 in the local area. But cast a wide net—include counties two over if you have to. I also need you to make sure they're AB negative."

"Oh—okay," Carter said, wincing. "Ummm... Should I do that now?"

"Carter, you should've done that five minutes ago."

The agent quickly nodded and gestured toward John. "Keys?" he said, wincing.

Agent Renee tossed the car keys to Carter and stood, watching as the young man scrambled into the front seat, did a fifteen-point turn to try to move out from behind another SUV, and then sped onto the road, lights flashing, pulling away and down the road.

Adele sighed, watching him go.

John frowned. He pointed one finger in the opposite direction of the car. "Isn't San Francisco that way?" he asked.

Adele nodded wearily. She watched as Carter reached the end of the road, then came to a screeching stop. He backed up, turned the vehicle, and came breezing past the other way, his eyes fixed determinedly on the road, refusing to look toward his captive audience, his cheeks tinged red through the open front window.

"How long of a drive back to the office?" John asked, muttering.

Adele shook her head. "An hour—too long."

"So we wait? Hope Carter can figure it out?"

Adele looked up at the darkening sky and massaged the back of her neck. "It is what it is," she said, softly. "Hopefully our killer waits until nightfall to strike."

Evening had already inserted itself across the horizon.

John glanced to Adele. "Work hours are almost done, yes? The roads will be clogged."

Adele shook her head. "Carter's not stupid. He'll be fine. I'm sure he will."

John pursed his lips, but didn't comment, turning away to move back toward the house and join the search while they waited for Agent Carter to reach the office and run their search.

Adele waited for John to step back into the house before quickly fishing her phone out and texting Carter. *"Use the shoulder and siren. Fast."*

Then she stood on the curb, beneath the dimming sky, waiting and watching the flickering blue and red lights dancing across her vision, reflecting off tinted glass and the windows of the houses lining the street.

An hour, maybe two. That's how long it would take to get the information they needed. She could only hope the killer didn't strike before then.

CHAPTER TWENTY EIGHT

"Got a car?" Adele asked from where she leaned in the broken and splintered doorway of Jonathan Davis's home. John took the porch steps in one stride and the floorboards creaked as he stopped in front of her.

He nodded. "Yeah—got a car but it comes with a chauffeur. They don't trust us with it."

"Guess your reputation precedes you," Adele muttered. Though she teased, her heart wasn't in it. Her eyes kept flicking down toward her phone which she clutched desperately in her hand.

"He call yet?"

She shook her head. Now, night had fallen complete, inserting itself across the sky. Already, she spotted other vehicles pulling into driveways as their residents returned from work.

Agent Renee also leaned against the splintered door, his legs crossed, extending across the threshold. A couple of cops tried to pass, waiting for him to move, but John stayed put.

"Excuse me, sir?" said the nearest officer.

John winced, tapped his ear and with an apologetic inflection, and said, in French, "Sorry, I don't speak English."

The officer scowled, but stepped over John's leg and moved down the porch toward the squad cars on the street.

Adele and John reclined in the splintered doorway, waiting, the atmosphere tense with anticipation. Adele didn't have it in her to strike up a conversation. Already, they were running late—she felt certain. The killer was on the move—hasty, desperate. The scene back in his basement suggested he hadn't even stopped to clean the shattered bottle and blood bag. Which meant he was acting rashly.

Adele still wasn't certain of the killer's motive. But with men like this, more and more, she was realizing how little she cared. It didn't matter *why* they killed—all that mattered was she stopped them. AB negative—wine of the same vintage year... It all ended with one conclusion: Jonathan Davis would kill another and another until she put him behind bars or placed a bullet between his eyes.

"Hear anything from Robert?" John asked, his voice low.

She glanced over and shook her head. Her eyes flicked back to her phone. The longer this case took, the longer it would be before she could see her old mentor. Would he still be alive by the end? "Come on," she muttered, shaking free of the oppressive thoughts. How long did it take Carter to drive back to the office and run a quick search? Adele twisted her fingers in frustration around the smooth glass surface of her phone, now warm from holding it so long.

Nearly an hour and a half had passed since the young agent had set off back to the agency. An hour and a half was a long time.

Adele pressed her head back against the door, closing her eyes and exhaling.

"Adele," John said.

"I haven't heard from him," she replied, curtly.

"No... wasn't going to say that," he continued hesitantly. "About... About our *talk*... in your room at the hotel... I just..."

Adele winced. *Not now,* she thought desperately. *Let's not talk about this now.*

As if in response to her urging thoughts, her phone suddenly began to buzz. Adele's fingers vibrated, prickling at the tips, and she looked down sharply as John fell silent also noting her reaction.

She read the name and quickly answered the phone. "Carter," she barked, her voice louder than she'd intended. "Tell me good news."

She heard Sam Carter on the other end, mumbling and bumbling a greeting, an introduction, but at last, he stammered out, "I-I worked with the files your friend at Interpol sent over. Lumen Relief has donors in the area. But they also have access to the names from other agencies—Red Cross, et cetera..."

"And?" Adele pressed. She now leaned forward, her head no longer pressed against the wood grain.

"And," Carter supplied, "I found five names. Five names in those birth years, with AB negative in a fifty-mile radius."

"Five?" Adele said, a prickle across the back of her hand. "That's... that's not many at all. Excellent—excellent work! Do you have numbers—addresses? We need to warn them—right now!"

"I'm sending the info now. Also sending it to dispatch for the backup with you."

"Excellent, perfect," Adele said, practically crowing. "Great work, Sam. I'm hanging up—send me the numbers. Now!"

She heard the line die, and then, a few moments later, her phone buzzed. She glanced around and noticed the officers standing by their vehicles answering their radios, or looking at their own phones as the notifications came up.

Adele scrolled to her messages, found the unmarked number, and opened the file. Five names, five addresses, five phone numbers.

"John," she said, wiggling her fingers. "Start calling. Right now— we have to warn them."

Hastily, John fished his phone out. He leaned in next to Adele, his breath warm and heavy against her cheek. Together, they parsed the numbers. Adele took the bottom three numbers and John took the top two.

After a moment, her fingers still prickling, Adele hastily dialed her first one. She heard John do the same. She waited, and the person in question picked up on the third ring.

"Hello?" said a voice on the other end. "Who is this?"

"My name is Agent Sharp," Adele rattled off, now stepping down the porch and into the lawn. "I'm with the FBI. I need you to listen closely."

"Is—is this a joke? Sal, is that you?" The voice seemed equal parts annoyed and amused. It creaked with age and Adele heard another voice in the background. "Who is it, Greg?" Adele tried to interject, but before she could, she heard a muffled voice replying, suggesting the phone had been pressed against someone's shirt.

She scowled in frustration, waiting expectantly. A moment later, the voice on the other end said, "All right, Sal—good one. I'm watching the game and you better believe I remember our wager."

"No, sir," Adele said quickly. "I really am with the FBI. You're in danger. I'll have an officer call you as well to confirm. I need you to stay inside, understand? You and anyone in your household. Lock the doors, don't talk to anyone."

A pause, a stretch of silence as the person on the other end seemed to be determining if she was serious or not.

"Sal?" the voice said hesitantly.

Adele swallowed back a shout. "No—I'm not Sal. My name is Adele Sharp. I work with Interpol, DGSI, and the FBI. You'll receive a confirmation call soon from local police. For now, though, it's imperative you listen to me. Stay inside, lock your doors, don't talk to anyone you don't know. Understand? Do you have family?"

The voice started to crack now, prickles of panic interjected into the tone. "Hang on, you're not joking?"

"No, sir. Look—I have others I need to call. Please, just follow my instructions."

"Wait—hang on, am I in danger?"

"I hope not. But possibly. Look, I need you to—"

"Is this connected to that body dropped over on Darby?"

Adele breathed heavily. "Yes sir," she said. "Please, just do as I say."

She heard another muffled sound as the phone was once again pressed to a shirt or a leg. A shrill voice now called out, "Honey—lock the doors! No, it's the police. I don't know. Yes, now!"

Adele waited, but the person didn't reply again. She waited a bit more, then hung up—it would have to do. At least, by the sound of things, it seemed as if they were complying with the directive. She had two other numbers to go.

The next two calls went a bit more smoothly. One of them, another local officer had already notified. Though they seemed panicked and badgered her with questions she couldn't answer, it felt as if at least they would take care for the night. A locked door wouldn't keep the killer out if he was determined, but it would help.

She looked at John. His voice had been a humming background noise up to this point. But now, as he cursed, muttering, *"Merde,"* a couple of times between breaths, she frowned. "What?" she asked.

He was looking at his phone, dialing a number and waiting. "No response," he said, growling. "They're not answering."

Adele looked over his shoulder. A local number, belonging to one Arthur Castle. In his sixties—lived alone.

She cursed and dialed the number herself. She waited—no response. She tried again, still no response.

"Stop," John snapped. "You might be blocking me from reaching him. Hang up—I'll try."

Adele complied and waited impatiently as John's fingers tapped the number. They both waited with bated breath in the wreath of splintered wood, watching the white numbers against the backdrop of blue.

"No answer," John cursed. He looked at her.

Adele was already moving down the porch and called, "Which car is ours?"

148

John followed quickly, pointing out the vehicle he'd managed to wrangle. "We're supposed to wait for an officer to come with—"

But Adele was already moving to the driver's side. Keys were in the ignition. She hopped in the front, waited for John to follow and, using the sound of the slamming door as a starter pistol, she gunned the engine.

"John, call Carter. Tell him to get the locals to head toward the addresses. I want at least two officers outside each house, understand?"

John nodded, already dialing.

Adele turned to face the windshield, grimacing and pulling away from the curb, maneuvering rapidly through the parked vehicles. She scraped against a mailbox and winced. She didn't have time for Agent Carter's patented fifteen-point turn, though. Paint on a car could be replaced, blood in a person would be far more difficult.

Why wasn't Mr. Castle answering? Was the killer with him already?

She slammed a hand into the steering wheel and, pulling past the final SUV blockading the side street, she glanced down, looking to the address and, with one trembling hand, programmed it into her phone's GPS. The device calculated the journey for far too long, in Adele's estimation, but at last, when she was on the verge of pulling hair, it began directing her toward Mr. Castle's home.

She could only hope they weren't already too late.

***

Adele jumped the curb, slammed the brakes, put the car in park, and hopped out, ignoring John's pointed look at the parking job. He followed close behind, clearing his throat, having spent the duration of the ten-minute trip advising officers to head toward the other potential victims.

Adele raced toward the small single-story beige cottage-shaped home. The paint job seemed fresh and the roof looked as if it had been recently replaced. A renovation? A strange thought—irrelevant, she decided.

Adele and John hastened along the sidewalk, across the lawn. A small asphalt roundabout led to the garage and then, along the front of the house and back to the street on the other side. She ignored the gray and trampled the green, reaching the door a step ahead of John.

149

"Mr. Castle?" she called, her voice loud. She pounded on the door with a clenched fist. "Mr. Castle?" she repeated, raising her voice even more now.

She glanced toward a nearby window. The lights were off inside.

"FBI!" John called, and pounded on the door as well, his massive fist sending tremors through the wood.

Still no response.

"Damn it," Adele muttered. She paced around the side of the house, looking for lights in the windows, for any sign of movement.

"Adele, I'm taking it down," John growled. He faced the door, breathing heavy and preparing himself. He took a couple of steps back, preparing to charge. Adele winced in anticipation, but just then, her phone began to ring.

"John!" she called sharply.

He pulled up, looking over at where she stood beneath one of the dark windows. A number without a name—the same number she'd been trying to call. "It's him!" she said, sharply. John still heaved a breath skyward, but, at least for now, he didn't rearrange the door.

She answered the phone. "Agent Sharp—is this Mr. Castle?"

A swallow, and then a dazed voice. "Did you say *Agent*?"

"Is this Mr. Castle?" she repeated. "I'm outside your home at 311 West Monroe. Sir, where are you?"

Another swallow, but then the man replied, "I'm—yes, this is Arthur Castle. Look—why are you at my house?"

"Sir, for your own safety, please—where are you?"

"I'm—I'm not home," he said, frowning. "I'm working late. What's this about? Is Jeremy okay?" he said, suddenly, his voice sharp.

"Sir, I don't know a Jeremy—"

"My son—he works in the city. Was he—"

"Your son is fine. This is about you, sir. Where are you, right now?"

"Work, I said."

"And where do you work?"

"I'm in real estate. I was showing a client an hour ago and I'm closing up. Why?"

Adele felt a shiver. "Are you on your own now?"

"Yes… The client left a while ago. What's this about?"

"Sir, I need you to stay exactly where you are. Tell me your address, please. We'll meet you there—I need you to stay put."

150

"Adele," John called from the front of the house, waving his phone at her.

She held up a finger, but he called more insistently.

She rounded on her partner, scowling. "What?"

He waved his phone and said, "Carter—the other potential victims are safe and accounted for. Uniforms outside their homes. Doors locked. Mr. Castle is the only one in the wind."

Adele cursed and returned her attention to her phone. "Mr. Castle, look, I know you're a blood donor, AB negative, I know you were born 1956. All right—I'm saying this not to scare you, but so you know I'm with the agency. I need you to tell me where you are, right this instant."

A pause—a precious pause. Adele knew at this very moment, he was deciding if he could trust her. She exhaled in frustration, closing her eyes and waiting.

And then the voice on the other end said, "214 East Sage Street. There's a key in a plastic stone out front. I'll be inside—I'll head to the basement. Can't you tell me what this is about?"

"I will, sir. Don't panic, but please do lock yourself in. Do not let *anyone* in. I mean it! Are the doors already locked?"

"The front is. But..." He trailed off and then his voice carried an edge. "I let the couple I was showing the house onto the back porch— they wanted to look at the bird feeders. I—I think I may have forgotten to lock it."

Adele bit her lip, but said, "Sir, please, do so now. Head to the basement and stay put. We're on our way."

Then she spun on John. "Others are all accounted for?"

He nodded. "Their babysitters will call if they get a glimpse of Mr. Davis."

"So they haven't? No sign of him?"

John winced and shook his head. He gestured airily toward her ear. "Was that our missing puzzle piece?"

Adele was already rushing back to the car. She was sick of driving, sick of GPS, sick of rushing place to place. It felt like they were still one step behind.

She felt a shivering sensation at the thought as she thrust into the driver's seat. One step behind... Just one step... But sometimes, one step was all a killer needed.

***

Arthur Castle lowered his phone, wrinkling his nose. He sighed softly and glanced along the dim glow from the light above the kitchen table. He hesitated for a moment, spotting a streak in the polish of the furniture. He frowned now, retrieving a paper towel and rubbing at the streak.

He hoped the clients hadn't seen it—this sale was an important one. Inwardly, he made a mental note to hire another cleaning service next time. Streaks on tables were unacceptable, especially given the amount he'd paid the cleaning crew.

Mr. Castle frowned, pausing for a moment and feeling his back begin to ache from where he bent over. He winced and straightened—he didn't move like he used to. His son, Jeremy, had often tried to convince him to retire. But Mr. Castle hated the very thought—what would he do all day? Watch TV, mull over crosswords? No thank you. He'd be selling houses until the day he died.

For a moment, all that mattered was the streak on the table. He rubbed at it, and even retrieved some soap, scrubbing the surface with a rag. He frowned—not much better. Maybe it was an imperfection in the wood itself. He'd have to see if he could still return the piece.

As he stood there, he felt a faint breeze across his neck and frowned. He looked up, glancing through the house. Such a strange phone call. He'd thought it had been a particularly zealous client given the volume of missed calls. He always kept his phone on silent when showing a house. Now, though, he began to move away from the table.

That was right, the loud lady had wanted him to lock the back door. Hadn't even bothered to tell him what this was about. Jeremy was a powerful attorney in San Francisco—and Mr. Castle was very proud of his son. If something had happened to his only child, he wasn't sure what he would do.

These thoughts troubled him as he moved slowly, carefully, along the hall toward the back sliding screen door which led into the backyard.

He paused for a moment, feeling another breeze across his face. Had he left a window open, too? The house was quite large—quite nice. It would be a big sale if he could manage it.

Then again, Mr. Castle was the third most prolific agent in the county. He smiled in pride at the thought and moved toward the back door before pulling up sharply.

152

His expression of satisfaction slowly morphed into a frown. He stared at the sliding glass. He'd suspected he'd forgotten to lock it—but he was near certain he hadn't left it open.

So why was the door ajar? The small plastic curtain partitions swept and swayed on the quiet nighttime breeze, clacking against each other and against the glass. Mr. Castle moved forward, his frown ever deepening. He reached out with a soft hand and held the door handle. For a moment he paused, peering out into the garden.

A flicker of movement.

He nearly yelped, but caught himself. And then laughed. A blue jay had landed in one of the bird feeders. The bird was pecking at the seed and flitting along the edge of the thing. Mr. Castle smiled for a moment, watching the bird. The bird feeders came with the house, a big selling point. A local carpenter had crafted them—intricate pieces of art, each one. And below, the spilling waterscape in the small pond created a serene foreground to the white wooden fence circling the yard.

He smiled at the bird, clicking his tongue to catch its attention. The bird glanced over, went stiff, then fluttered off.

Mr. Castle chuckled and watched the creature flit away, searching for more private feeding grounds. Then he stepped back into the house fully and slid the glass door shut. He locked the door and slowly turned. The agent had told him to wait here. Wait he would.

He glanced along the hall toward the basement door and began to move toward it.

He frowned—why could he still feel a breeze? His gaze moved toward the dining room, next to the sliding glass door. Dark, no lights, but a window was open. A window on the side of the house facing the woods.

He felt a trickle of fear now seeping down his neck.

And then a form suddenly emerged from beneath the dining table. A man, clad in black, rushing forward. Mr. Castle cried out, tried to protect himself. He glimpsed blue eyes, then a swiping hand. And then he felt something hard, like iron, slam into his throat.

His eyes went sightless—black spots—streaks of white pain.

Then nothing.

CHAPTER TWENTY NINE

Adele strode past the *For Sale* sign in the front yard. She gestured toward John to hasten after her. Both of them moved quietly, and John dropped into a crouch, his firearm in his hands. They reached the front door and Adele put her hand on the brass knob.

John looked at her, waiting.

"Locked," she mouthed.

John mimed kicking, but Adele shook her head. She held up a finger and fished her phone from her pocket. She returned the most recent call and waited, watching the windows, her eyes on the house, looking for any reaction.

None was forthcoming.

John kept his eyes fixed on her, waiting, watching.

She held up a cautioning finger and tried the number again. Still no answer—no ring. She felt a prickle along her spine.

"I don't think we should knock," she said, in a nearly inaudible whisper.

John pressed against the nearest window, his eye against a crack between the wall outside and the drapes within.

"Anything?" she whispered.

He shook his head.

Adele nodded, took stock of the house, and her eyes slid around the brown siding toward a small green gate set between the house and a large, white fence. She gestured at John, pointing, and together, they stepped off the porch and moved, quietly, cautiously, circling around the house. Adele opened the gate, wincing as it creaked on tired hinges.

She sidled along the house, taking quick and hurried steps along the stones set in the grass and ground. She moved around the back of the house and spotted three bird feeders lined over a small pond.

John, though, hadn't stopped at the spectacle and instead was gesturing wildly at her. She followed his gaze toward an open window on the first floor next to a large glass sliding door.

For a moment, Adele frowned and then she heard John curse. His weapon shot up and he pointed straight at the window.

"Put the knife down!" he shouted, his voice blasting next to Adele like a cannon.

For a moment, disoriented, she struggled to place the source of his consternation, and then, through the open window, she spotted it. A man was stooped over a still form pressed to a dining room table. The upright fellow had a plastic bag clutched in one hand and a knife in the other. The bag extended to a tube which curled around and around, resting against the back of a chair before ending in a needle inserted into the other form's arm.

"Damn it!" Adele shouted. "Get down!" she screamed. "Drop the knife!"

John aimed and fired, two shots. He hadn't been aiming through the window, though, on account of possibly hitting the victim. Instead, he shot the glass sliding door.

The shards hung suspended for a moment, displaying all manner of cracks and facets, and then they rained down, collapsing with a mighty crash across the deck and into the house.

Adele was already stumbling through the opening, her own weapon clutched cold and firm in her palms. She pointed the firearm toward the man by the table.

"Jonathan Davis, lower the knife!"

The man still held his blade aloft, staring at her, a crazed look in his eyes. He swallowed, emitting a dry sound so loud that Adele could practically hear it echo. She watched his Adam's apple bob and he pressed his blade hard into the skin of the other form on the table.

Now in the house, hearing John curse and growl as he maneuvered over scattered glass, she got a good look at the victim.

Mr. Castle, she presumed. An older gentleman, his eyes closed, his face and skin pale, slick. The IV in his arm continued to pump blood into the bag gripped in Mr. Davis's other hand.

"Drop the knife, now!" Adele shouted, angling for a shot.

But Mr. Davis, still breathing heavily, his eyes still widened, shifted, following her steps and keeping his victim between himself and the agents.

"Back!" Davis spat. He had pulsing blue eyes and features that would have been handsome if not for the crazed sheen over his countenance. "Get back!" he screamed, waving his knife threateningly beneath his victim's chin.

"Drop it!" John's voice boomed.

Davis was gasping and spitting now, looking to the window next to him, glancing frantically around the dining room, seemingly in search of some escape route.

"Don't even try it," Adele snarled. "Mr. Davis, lower the knife, or I'll shoot!"

He looked at her now, for a moment seemingly forgetting the blood bag. "Do you really mean it?" he asked, a tinge of hope to his voice. "You would send me south? Would you pay the river fare? Hmm?"

Adele blinked. She didn't look at John, but could sense his confusion as well as he shifted cautiously along the hall in a half-step, his weapon still pinpointing the murderer.

"Sir, we can talk about it—just lower the knife."

Mr. Davis licked his lips, a pink tongue darting out and slipping across dry flesh like a lizard.

"You don't understand," he said, snorting now as if trying to breathe and swallow at the same time. He gasped. "I need this—I need it. I must—must strengthen my spirit. It's the code, I'm sure of it now. This is Gabriel's number—he'll usher me home. I know he will!"

John made a quiet whistling sound next to Adele's ear.

"I'm not crazy!" Mr. Davis screamed now, pointing the knife toward John.

For a moment, Adele felt like he'd presented an opportunity, but just as quickly, he ducked behind a chair, cursing, hiding from line of sight.

"Mr. Davis, I'm sure you're not," Adele said, scowling. "Now lower that blade and we can all get out of this in one piece."

"That's just it!" he howled from behind the table. "Too many pieces—not one. Too many! Fractured and tethered souls, bound to this plane by fear and ailment. I march the sojourner's path! I march onward!"

Then she heard a deep sucking noise. For a moment, Adele frowned. She glanced at the victim, who still seemed to be breathing, thank goodness, his chest rising in slow, shallow motions. But then her eyes widened as she glanced at the blood bag. It lay discarded on the table, dappling the oak with a smattering of droplets. The tube from the IV, though, was out of sight—no longer attached to the bag.

Adele felt a cold shiver and sidestepped now around the table, moving deeper into the dining room and gesturing for John to do the

156

same. She went still.

Mr. Davis was ducked behind the chair still and had the tube in his lips. He was sucking it, swallowing deeply and giggling as he flooded himself, drinking the victim's blood like from a straw.

Adele felt sick, but she steeled herself and pointed her weapon at Mr. Davis. Aimed, and fired.

But he was quick. He spotted her, spat the tube out and rolled under the table, avoiding the blast. The blood now pooled on the varnished ground, staining against the Turkish rug beneath the table. The victim on top of the table let out a quiet little gasp.

Adele glanced toward where Mr. Davis was scrambling out the other side, her eyes flicking toward John, then to the victim. She lunged forward, ripping the tube from Mr. Castle's arm and tossing it to the side. She grabbed a cloth placemat set in the center of the table and quickly discarded it as too thick.

Cursing to herself, desperate, she pulled her own pocket lining and ripped, hard. Then, using this, she pressed it firmly to Mr. Castle's arm. "Mr. Castle," she said, "Arthur, listen to me. Stay awake—Arthur you're going to be fine. Stay with me!" She practically was yelling now, watching Mr. Castle's eyes flutter in his wizened face. He was older than Robert, but not by much. She could feel panic setting in as she desperately reached for her phone, placing her gun on the table so she could call for paramedics.

John had his own weapon raised, but a second later, a chair was knocked free from beneath the table and sent slamming into the tall agent. He went down with a howl. Mr. Davis darted forward now, tackling John around the ankles, but then, just as quickly, using it as a feint to switch his strike.

A hand leapt out as quick and powerful as a piston. He struck John in the throat.

The tall French agent gave a gasping, gurgling nose. His hands darted to his neck and his gun dropped, clattering to the ground.

Adele shouted incoherently, one hand holding a makeshift bandage to the victim's still bleeding arm, another pressing a phone to her ear as she desperately called for paramedics.

"Ambulance, now!" she screamed when she heard a response on the other line. There was no more time. She dropped her phone, allowing it to hit the ground and crash amidst the pooling blood at her feet. Her shoes were also stained at this point.

157

But it didn't matter. She snatched her weapon off the table, aimed, and tried to fire again.

But John had recovered enough to tackle Mr. Davis, who was bolting toward the shattered sliding door. John was making a wheezing hacking sound like a cat with a hairball. Mr. Davis spun around where he was knocked to the floor. He snarled and lashed out again—fast, deadly. His fingers aimed for John's eyes.

But this time, the French agent seemed to be expecting it. He didn't speak, but spat, jerking his head to the side and using the momentum to slam his forehead square into Mr. Davis's groin.

Adele winced and Mr. Davis went stiff as a board, squeaking in agony. John surged up now, dragging Mr. Davis by the collar and flinging him into a cabinet, sending the killer crashing head-first into the wood.

But Mr. Davis was like a cornered animal. He was the smaller man, but the more desperate one. He raised a hand, which, miraculously, still held the knife Adele had spotted earlier. With a howl, he charged at John, slashing at the big man's face—again, it seemed, going for the eyes.

"You're blind!" Mr. Davis screeched. "Blind!"

John ducked one way, then surged back, distancing himself, trying to circle toward his firearm. But even in this crazed state, Mr. Davis seemed to realize the large agent's intent; he circled as well, keeping John between Adele and himself, but also cutting off access to the agent's gun in the kitchen.

John tried to step forward, but Mr. Davis wiggled the knife threateningly.

For a moment, they stood, facing each other, the smaller, bloodstained man carrying a knife, the taller one gasping and glancing around the kitchen, trying to find another angle.

"You big freak," Mr. Davis spat, "I've got you. You're going nowhere, understand? Now hear my terms. I'll let you leave, but only if—"

John was not in a listening mood. He seemed to resign himself to the inevitable. And then, instead of trying to dodge the knife, he surged toward it. One meaty fist snared the blade around the edge. Mr. Davis howled, yanking his weapon. A spurt of blood, but John managed to hang on, gripping the knife by the very blade. The tall agent howled in pain, but then jerked, yanking the weapon free where it had embedded

158

into his palm.

Adele just stared.

Mr. Davis didn't seem to believe what had just happened.

"Here are *my* terms," John snarled. He flung out a hand, scattering droplets of blood from his freshly injured palm into Mr. Davis's eyes, distracting him for a second. And then he surged forward, grabbing the killer by the throat, lifting him and tossing him like a child across the kitchen into the refrigerator with a loud *thud!*

There was a crunching noise and Mr. Davis went very still.

Breathing heavily, with blood staining his shirt from where Mr. Davis had spat on him, John turned, looking at Adele, his eyes wide and feral as they often got in situations like this. Blood trickled between his curled fingers where he'd snared the blade, pattering to the carpet at his feet. He blinked, shook his head, and said, "That was close."

Adele began to speak, but then screamed.

John spun around. Mr. Davis had recovered Agent Renee's gun. He pointed the weapon at the Frenchman. Aimed for the head.

A gunshot.

Mr. Davis slumped over, his hand falling limp, lifeless to the tiled kitchen floor. Adele's own weapon was raised, trembling in her grip, pointed at the killer and emitting a soft puff of smoke. Her other hand still gripped the bandage against Mr. Castle, and between her feet, she could hear a voice squawking on the other end of the discarded phone, calling out her name.

She stood over the pool of blood, still gripping her weapon and staring at John with unblinking eyes.

The French agent reached up and pressed delicately against his cheek. He licked his lips and pulled his hand away. A thin, faint trail of blood laced his cheek.

"W-was that me?" Adele said, hyperventilating. "Was that my bullet?"

John's fingers were steady, his tone without inflection. "Think so," he said, lowering his blood-tipped fingers. "Another scar, I suppose. Thanks to my American Princess." He glanced toward where Mr. Davis leaned against the cabinets, a bullet between his eyes.

John whistled. "Nice shot."

"I—I almost hit you," Adele said, still breathing heavily.

John probed at his cut cheek and winced. "Technically, I think you did. Don't worry," he said, his voice shaking for the first time. "I won't

159

tell if you don't."

Adele just stared incredulously past her partner at the fallen form of Mr. Davis. His eyes were still open, his hand splayed on either side of him, his mouth stained with blood which had dripped down his neck in sticky streaks of crimson, dabbing his shirt collar.

He had the faintest of smiles on his face as his lifeless eyes stared directly at Adele. For a moment, he almost seemed at peace—his features arranged into a look of lifeless gratitude. But then Adele shuddered, looked away, and turned all her attention on Mr. Castle.

She murmured, "It's going to be okay. Sir, stay with me. Help is on the way." Then, louder, she lifted her head and called, "Christ, John, I don't know if he's going to make it. Make sure the ambulance is coming. Now!"

John nodded at her, his phone already in his hand, the number already dialed. He turned away, took two strides toward Mr. Davis's form, and kicked the firearm skittering across the ground. He moved over, retrieved the weapon and pocketed it, speaking in low, urgent tones.

CHAPTER THIRTY

Adele and John sat at the edge of a small, makeshift pond, beneath three bird feeders. Night had fallen but the lights set up by the paramedics and the crime scene unit cast a haze across the backyard. Still, beneath the warm glare of the lights, witnessing the movement through the house, Adele sat, shivering, shaking.

John glanced at her, his eyes half-hooded, a bandage now wrapped around his mangled hand.

"Gotta stop hurting my shooting hand," he muttered. "Third time since we've been partnered."

Adele returned his look. She exhaled deeply. "Second time," she muttered. "Don't exaggerate, you big baby."

She'd meant it as a joke, but as the words left her lips she felt a flash of guilt. Her eyes darted to John's cheek. He hadn't accepted a bandage for the shallow graze from Adele's bullet. The same bullet that had taken Mr. Davis.

She shuddered, looking at the streak of red against her partner's face, and looked away again, her eyes flicking back to the house.

She watched as paramedics emerged, moving carefully, gently, carrying Mr. Castle out on a stretcher and around the side of the house. She heard the paramedics instructing each other, guiding their team safely and cautiously along the stone path.

Careful was good. Careful meant he was still alive.

"You got here in time," John murmured, nodding past Adele's hunched form toward the paramedics.

She didn't reply, still trembling and shaking.

John reached out, putting an arm around her shoulder and pulling her close. For a moment, she stiffened, her eyes darting to the officers moving through the house, visible through the window. She heard quiet murmurs, radio chatter, and watched officers move delicately around the blood-spattered table and floor. She heard a commanding officer's voice call out from within, "Careful—no, back, back. Too many of you. Get back!"

She looked back toward the grass between her feet, swallowing a

161

breath of the cool night air of Sonoma County.

"You all right?" John asked after a moment.

She leaned a bit into him now, her shoulders relaxing somewhat. His injured hand draped past her right arm, his bandaged palm reflecting off the surface of the small pond. Above, she heard a twittering, rustling sound and looked up to see a small blue jay probing tentatively among the seeds.

"Pretty late for you, isn't it?" she murmured to the creature.

But the bird ignored her attention, seemingly emboldened by all the noise serving as a distraction so it could make good its pillaging of the free seed. Then, after a few more flutters of its wings, it darted away, moving off into the night.

Adele shook her head, smiling wryly. "Didn't know they fed this late."

John grunted. "Some birds don't let expectations define their decisions."

Adele glanced back at her partner, scowling at the side of his cheek. "Are you trying to be clever, John?"

He crossed his good hand over his heart and kissed the fingers. "Wouldn't dream of it."

Adele sighed, blinking, her eyes strained from the bright lights lining the backyard and emanating from within the house. "I'm tired," she murmured.

"I can drive back," John said. "If you trust me not to crash."

"I don't, but fine…"

Despite this, she made no move to rise. There was something comforting, safe, about sitting next to her partner, shivering, but warmed by his body heat. She leaned her head against his shoulder fully now.

He seemed to breathe a bit quieter, as if fearful he might disturb her, or startle her away. For now, though, she didn't care if anyone saw them, if it somehow got back to Foucault or Ms. Jayne. For now, she was simply tired and wanted to rest.

"Adele," John said, softly.

"Hmm? What do you think we should do with Mr. Davis's nephew? Carter was asking."

Adele hesitated a moment, closing her eyes to think. She heard the soft, artificial swish of the pond water lapping against the side of the stone basin. Then she shrugged. "Cut him loose. I don't think he had

162

anything to do with it."

"Even after covering for the killer?"

"His uncle. Family. The same uncle who would have been happy to let the boy take the fall for him. I think Ken will figure that out soon enough." Adele shook her head. "Yeah, let him go. He didn't know— was just trying to protect family."

John sniffed. "Fine. I'll tell Carter. You sure?"

"I'm sure. People risk a lot for family."

John breathed in a way that might have been a chuckle or might have been a sigh of resignation. She didn't bother to look up and see.

"Adele?" he said after another few moments of watching the movement through the windows.

"Yeah?"

"I like you."

She kept her eyes closed, still leaning against John, but a small smile twisted the corners of her lips. "I like you too," she said, softly.

"I'm shit poor with this sort of thing," John said.

Adele's smile remained. "Me too."

"Foucault?"

"I don't care. We'll tread carefully."

John snorted. "Not sure either of us knows how to do that."

Adele's eyes blinked open. Instead of replying, her gaze scanned the smashed window of the sliding door, slipped along the bloodstained hall, took in the scene of the police officers moving through the house, scouring the scene of carnage within.

"Yeah," she said. "Maybe not. Oh well."

John went quiet for a moment, then reiterated. "Oh well," the tall agent murmured to himself and then, louder, said, "I miss France."

Adele nodded, her hair shifting against the fabric of his shirt. "Yeah, me too."

"Let's go home."

Adele closed her eyes again. She wasn't entirely sure where home was. But for the moment, in the warmth of John's company, facing the distant gleam of flashing lights from an ambulance which carried Mr. Castle, alive, safe... she felt perhaps it didn't matter so much.

"Let's go home," she said.

163

CHAPTER THIRTY ONE

Executive Foucault had called her that morning and told her the news. Robert was awake. He wanted to talk.

The cab from the airport reached the hospital in record time. She glanced back where she stood on the sidewalk, watching the taxi peel away, doing an illegal U-turn and heading back in the direction of the airport.

She took the steps outside the hospital, quickly, as if wanting to get it over with as soon as possible. She reached the large sliding doors, beneath the symbol of a red heart in a curling stethoscope. She glanced off to the side, toward the roundabout near the emergency room. It didn't feel right arriving in a different way than her mentor. They'd been through a lot together.

That lump in her throat only seemed to worsen, and she swallowed, clearing it, stepping into the hospital. She moved quickly to the counter and addressed the nurse. "I'm here to see Agent Henry. I'm DGSI." She flashed her credentials, moving through the motions in robotic fashion.

The nurse looked at her, curious, but then glanced at the credentials, and nodded.

"Second floor," she said.

Adele hurried over to the elevator. Her eyes flicked to the stairs, but there were so many of them. So she waited for the metal box of death to ding, indicating it had arrived. The doors parted, and a couple stepped out. Adele waited for them to pass, breathing shallowly lest she absorb germs. And then she stepped into the elevator. She covered her hand with a sleeve and touched the button to the second floor. On the side of the elevator, etched into the metal, different descriptions of the floors informed her the second floor was for cancer.

"Dammit," she said as she stared at the word.

The doors dinged open far too soon. She found she even missed the elevator. But then, like a prisoner facing the gallows, she marched out of the elevator and moved along a desk and down a long hall.

A nurse in a green uniform, with her mouth covered, paused and

164

glanced back. Through her mask, her voice muffled, she said, "Can I help you?"

Adele shrugged. "Here to see Agent Henry. I was told he's on this floor."

The nurse hesitated, glanced at her clipboard, then looked down the hall. Then her eyes brightened. "Oh, you mean Robert?"

Something about the cheerful tone gave Adele a flash of hope. "Yes, is he here?"

The nurse nodded quickly. "Of course. Yes, come, I'll take you to him."

Adele suppressed a rare smile. It was just like Robert to start making friends, even in a hospital. The small, mustached Frenchman had a way of charming people.

She followed after the nurse, down the hall, moving past a doctor who seemed to be relaying news to a woman outside a glass door. They reached the end of the hall and Adele was ushered into a bright room with a large window.

The nurse smiled at Adele and said, "Give me a call if you need anything." And then, louder, "Robert, you have a guest!"

A familiar voice called out, "How delightful."

The nurse giggled and waved, then moved back through the doors, leaving Adele.

Robert had been looking out the window and for a moment, she stared at the back of his neatly combed head. Then her old mentor turned, his eyes vibrant. When he saw who was waiting for him in the room his smile only brightened.

He looked at her, his eyes tender. His face was gaunt, his cheeks sickly pale. His chest pressed against hospital robes seemed little more than bones and skin.

"Oh dear," Adele said, finding tears suddenly springing up and slipping down her face. "Oh dear," she repeated. It felt like she couldn't think of another word. "Oh," she said, exhaling deeply, "dear."

Robert just looked at her, his gaunt face pressed against his pillow. He was sitting upright, and he watched her as she wept. "Don't cry, my darling," he said, softly. "See, they gave me a room with a window. I asked, and they moved me."

Adele took a couple of stumbling steps forward, allowing her luggage to fall from her fingertips and thump against the floor. She approached Robert and reached out, squeezing at his hand. "Robert,

Robert," she said, wheezing.

"There, there," he said, softly, caressing the back of her hand with his thumb. He smiled at her, warmth emanating from his gaze. He leaned over and kissed the back of her hand.

"Robert, what's the matter? Why didn't you tell me?"

Robert held her hand and pressed his other against it. His fingers were so very frail, his grip so very weak.

"Darling Adele," he said, softly, "you always want to know everything." He chuckled. "It's what makes you such a great investigator."

"Robert, you should've told me."

He shook his head. "I didn't know."

She stared at him. "How couldn't you know? You've been coughing, and I've seen—"

"I didn't want to know. I could sense," he said, nodding at her, smiling softly. "I could sense I was nearing the end of my story. But I didn't want to know how. That's cheating. Looking in the back of the book." He chuckled.

And for a moment, as he reclined back and gave a small, satisfied sigh, Adele thought of his red leather chair, facing the fire in his study. She thought of the pile of books upon the coffee table next to him. She thought of the long conversations they would have at night, well into the morning, staring at the burning blaze turning to ash.

She thought of his warmth, his hugs, his laughter. She thought of the cupboard full of chocolate cereal he kept just for her. The plastic bowls he'd bought just to match the one her mother had once gifted her.

She thought of his invitations to his mansion, giving her freedom to live in his house as if it were her own.

"How bad is it?" she said.

Robert gave a little cough. He shook his head. "They say it's half the size of a football," he chuckled sharply.

She stared.

"Ironic, isn't it?" he said. "I lost my teeth in a football match, you know." He reached up and pointed at his missing teeth.

"I thought you said they were taken out in a boxing match in Belarus."

Robert waved airily. "That happened too."

"The tumor is that big?"

"Three of them," he said, "in fact. But they're going to try to operate this weekend."

Adele felt a flicker of hope. "And?"

He shrugged. "Went from my stomach and hit my lymph nodes. Seems like even if they had caught it months ago, it wouldn't matter."

Adele felt the hope leave her, draining from her and leaving her gaunt like blood sucked from one of Mr. Davis's victims. "How long do you have?" she said, breathlessly.

Robert rubbed his thumb across her knuckles again. "That would be reading the back of the book," he said. "I don't know."

"Robert, this isn't a book. It's your life. I need you," she said, her voice cracking. "I can't do this without you."

Robert looked at her, and for the first time since she'd entered the room his smile failed completely and tears began to spill from his own eyes.

He looked at her and held her gaze. There was a bravery there, an unwillingness to look away. "Adele," he said, his voice firm, "you're stronger than you think."

She shook her head, now blubbering, feeling snot bubbles forming and tears slipping down her cheeks. She knew she looked a mess, but this was the one person for whom it didn't matter. He wouldn't care what she looked like. "Robert, I can't. You can't go. Please," she said, desperately. "Please, you need to stay."

Robert looked at her, and then he coughed. He leaned back and inhaled, drawing in air. "Adele, all of us leave eventually."

"I know that."

He looked at her. "You never did. It's why you have this job. You think you can stop it. My dear, my lovely, precious, beautiful, wonderful child. You think you can stop it."

She looked at him. "This can't be it."

Robert chuckled. "Some say it isn't. Executive Foucault was down here yesterday. I gave him the satisfaction of a prayer."

Adele winced and smiled despite herself, despite the tears, despite her snotty nose. "He had you pray?"

Robert grinned at her now, and wagged his head. "It didn't particularly make me feel better, but it did seem to help him."

Adele gave an ugly, snorting bark of laughter. She didn't care, though. "Are you scared?"

Robert shook his head. "No, darling. In our job, if you spend so much time around death, it eventually loses its bite."

She looked at him and shivered. She remembered where she was standing. A hospital. She thought of her mother. She thought of the last case. She stared at her old mentor, and all the humor had bled from her voice. "Not for me," she whispered.

Robert looked at her and patted her hand. "I know. I know. But eventually," he said, quiet, "eventually, the fear goes away."

"Why? How could it?"

"Adele," he said, looking at her.

"What?" She wasn't as brave as him. She couldn't meet his eyes. She kept her hand extended, pressed against his blankets, feeling the soft touch of his grip. But she simply couldn't look him in the eyes.

He said, "This matters."

She glanced down. "I know."

But he gave her hand a little jerk. "No, listen to me. This matters. It hurts. And so, it matters."

"I know that," she said.

He held her hand, though, firmly now. "You're not hearing me. Your life matters. Maybe the Executive is right. And maybe we meet again. Maybe he's wrong, and maybe this is dust to dust, nothing to nothing. But I need you to promise me you're not going to fall for the lie that you can't do this. There are others who will love you, Adele. Listen to me. No, don't pull away, listen. This is important. If there's one thing you hear from me, this is it. I'm not the only one that will love you in your life—you have my promise. That's impossible. There are so many that will find love for you. But you have to give them the chance. Understand? Don't be afraid to love first. Don't you dare. While there's life, while it lasts, that's when it matters."

She looked at him. "You're talking like you're dead already."

He smiled. "Not yet. Not quite yet. Adele, you can do this. I know you've lost so much." He sobbed now, suddenly, the sound shaking in the room. "You lost too much. And it isn't fair. But there's just as much love to replace that which was taken. You save so many lives. You've helped so many families. People who could've had mothers taken. Daughters taken. Brothers, sons, fathers. You stopped it. But now, you need to promise me one thing."

Adele looked at him, and just waited.

"You have to help yourself. Let it go. Let it go."

"Let what go?" she whispered.

He stared her straight in the eyes. "You know what. Please, for my sake, for yours, let it go. And call your father, Adele. Life is too short."

Her father... she hadn't thought of him in a while, since their falling out. Adele felt like she had a headache now. Robert wasn't making much sense. At least, she didn't think he was. Perhaps that was part of the cancer. She just nodded, hoping perhaps this would put him at ease. He leaned back in the pillows now and patted her hand again. "Go," he said, "you don't need to stay. I like looking out the window."

Adele snorted. "You better believe I'm staying through the night."

Robert chuckled. "I'm not sure they'll let you."

Adele grunted. "Yeah? You're a wanted fugitive. I have to keep an eye on you. If they try to prevent me, they're breaking the law. So there."

Robert was chuckling so hard now he began to cough, and it sent his body shaking painfully.

Adele watched her old mentor, each of the retching sounds sending a bolt of agony through her own chest. She moved over toward the chair next to his bed. She sat down and pressed her hand against his, holding it.

It was still the afternoon. Hours, or hours after, it didn't matter. She would stay the night. And God help any nurse or doctor who tried to get her to leave.

CHAPTER THIRTY TWO

Adele ended up staying two days at the hospital. Twice, a doctor tried to get her to leave—the first time had required her badge, the second, her pistol. Eventually, though, they'd left her in peace. However, Adele felt certain that it was more due to their fondness for Robert rather than anything she'd said that allowed them to bend the rules.

They spent the time as they often had, talking, sitting side by side. It wasn't the same as leather chairs facing a fire, but they did end up finding a TV station that mimicked a fireplace. They left it on well into the night. Nurses had tried to insist Robert get his sleep, but Agent Henry had refused. And though Adele had tried to insist as well, he'd scolded her and then launched into another story about how the agency used to be in "the good old days."

Adele had listened, tears perpetually in her eyes. By the second day, she'd stopped crying. Not because she didn't want to cry, or because the sadness had left, but because sheer exhaustion and dehydration seemed to have dried her tears.

Now, she'd promised to return after a shower and a meal besides hospital food. Robert had insisted. Secretly, she suspected he hadn't wanted her around for palliative treatment. And though she hated herself for it, she hadn't wanted to be there.

Exhaustion lay heavy, accompanied by its close friends, shame and guilt, as she trudged up her apartment steps, her carry-on clutched in one tired hand. Too many emotions over the last few days. Laughter, tears—now, all Adele wanted to do was sleep for a year.

She marched up the steps, dragging her carry-on bumping against each marble slab. She passed her landlord's unit and smiled down the banister toward it. The old lady in 1A was a feisty woman—she'd helped on a case before. Or, at least, had tried to.

Adele reached her own unit, curling up the stairs and coming to a stop in front of the brown door.

She placed her bag on the ground, huffing a sigh and feeling the weight of anxiety lift as it was wont to do when near one's home.

But her breath caught. She frowned.

Bent over.

Something was on the doormat.

She stooped now, bending at the knee, some of the exhaustion fading to be replaced by a prickle of curiosity.

Not just that, but the curiosity was quickly replaced by a sudden jolt. She looked sharply up and down the hall. Empty. She hadn't seen anyone on the stairs. She cursed and sprinted toward the next flight, looking up; no one.

She glanced warily, trembling now, her eyes flitting to her neighbors' doors. None were open. No one was watching.

She turned, slowly, like in a horror movie when someone faced a ghost. Her eyes fixed on the item next to her carry-on, left on the doormat.

A Carambar. The same candy her mother had loved so dearly.

Trembling, her knees weak, she approached. Days lacking sleep, shedding tears, panic, all swirled through her at once. And her fingertips shook as she reached out and picked up the candy.

Still shaking, she pulled on either end of the wrapper, watching it twirl open. She spotted words written in marker on the inside. She gently lowered the candy onto her carry-on, careful not to touch too much of it—hard to lift a print, but possible.

She held the Carambar in a shivering grasp and stared at the words scrawled in blocky handwriting inside the candy wrapper.

I miss her too.

Adele yelled and threw the wrapper toward her door. It flicked and fluttered like a leaf on the wind and then drifted slowly to the ground, curling up one last time before settling just beneath the door.

She stared at the writing, her eyes blazing, her teeth set. Some of the dull, dreary emotions from the week began to fade, replaced now by an excited prickle along her spine.

She'd been on the right track. The killer had been spooked. He thought he was taunting her, playing with her—but he'd just made his first huge mistake.

She stared at the wrapper, breathing heavily, her fingers still shaking as she reached for her phone.

But just then, as if sensing her attention, the phone began to ring.

Adele frowned, staring down at her side, and then, as if in slow motion, she reached for the device and picked it up. For half a second, she expected the call to be coming from her mother's killer. But no—the office. Foucault's number.

"Sir?" she said, swallowing back any ounce of emotion.

"Agent Sharp?" said a voice on the other end.

Not Foucault, though. A female voice. It took Adele a second to realize it was Agent Sophie Paige.

"Yes?" Adele said.

"You're back in France?" said Agent Paige. Sophie's voice lacked its usual latent hostility. Which only sent another tremble through Adele's body.

"Paris, yes," said Adele, curt, her eyes still fixed on the Carambar.

"I—I don't know how to say this," Paige said, slowly. "But you're going to want to see this."

"See what?"

"A murder," said Paige.

"So soon?" said Adele. "Just got back from the hospital, is it—"

"It's my case—that's not why. Look, Adele... I know the timing is poor. But this body... Whoever killed them..." Agent Paige struggled to find the words, but then she said. "It's identical to your mother's murder. You should come by."

Adele stood quietly for a moment, closing her eyes and then opening them again, fixating on the Carambar. For a moment, it all felt like a dream. She felt certain she hadn't heard Paige correctly. Was she joking?

"Adele?" said Agent Paige. "Did you hear me?"

Adele didn't blink, didn't hesitate, and with a voice that snapped like a bear trap, she said, "Tell me where. I'm on my way."

NOW AVAILABLE!

LEFT TO ENVY
(An Adele Sharp Mystery—Book 6)

"When you think that life cannot get better, Blake Pierce comes up with another masterpiece of thriller and mystery! This book is full of twists and the end brings a surprising revelation. I strongly recommend this book to the permanent library of any reader that enjoys a very well written thriller."
--Books and Movie Reviews, Roberto Mattos (re Almost Gone)

LEFT TO ENVY is book #6 in a new FBI thriller series by USA Today bestselling author Blake Pierce, whose #1 bestseller Once Gone (Book #1) (a free download) has received over 1,000 five star reviews.

In the Sistine Chapel, the first tourists of the day look up—and are horrified to find a dead body affixed by ropes to the ceiling.

More victims soon appear, strung up in similarly dramatic fashion on other major attractions throughout Europe.

Who is killing them? Why? Who will be next?

And is FBI Special Agent Adele Sharp—triple agent of the U.S., France and Germany—brilliant enough to enter the serial killer's mind and stop him before it's too late?

An action-packed mystery series of international intrigue and riveting suspense, LEFT TO ENVY will have you turning pages late into the night.

Book #7 in the series—LEFT TO LAPSE—is now also available.

LEFT TO ENVY
(An Adele Sharp Mystery—Book 6)

Did you know that I've written multiple novels in the mystery genre? If you haven't read all my series, click the image below to download a series starter!

Blake Pierce

Blake Pierce is the USA Today bestselling author of the RILEY PAGE mystery series, which includes seventeen books. Blake Pierce is also the author of the MACKENZIE WHITE mystery series, comprising fourteen books; of the AVERY BLACK mystery series, comprising six books; of the KERI LOCKE mystery series, comprising five books; of the MAKING OF RILEY PAIGE mystery series, comprising six books; of the KATE WISE mystery series, comprising seven books; of the CHLOE FINE psychological suspense mystery, comprising six books; of the JESSE HUNT psychological suspense thriller series, comprising fourteen books (and counting); of the AU PAIR psychological suspense thriller series, comprising three books; of the ZOE PRIME mystery series, comprising four books (and counting); of the new ADELE SHARP mystery series, comprising six books (and counting); of the new EUROPEAN VOYAGE cozy mystery series, comprising six books (and counting); and of the new LAURA FROST FBI suspense thriller.

An avid reader and lifelong fan of the mystery and thriller genres, Blake loves to hear from you, so please feel free to visit www.blakepierceauthor.com to learn more and stay in touch.

BOOKS BY BLAKE PIERCE

LAURA FROST FBI SUSPENSE THRILLER
ALREADY GONE (Book #1)
ALREADY SEEN (Book #2)
ALREADY TRAPPED (Book #3)

EUROPEAN VOYAGE COZY MYSTERY SERIES
MURDER (AND BAKLAVA) (Book #1)
DEATH (AND APPLE STRUDEL) (Book #2)
CRIME (AND LAGER) (Book #3)
MISFORTUNE (AND GOUDA) (Book #4)
CALAMITY (AND A DANISH) (Book #5)
MAYHEM (AND HERRING) (Book #6)

ADELE SHARP MYSTERY SERIES
LEFT TO DIE (Book #1)
LEFT TO RUN (Book #2)
LEFT TO HIDE (Book #3)
LEFT TO KILL (Book #4)
LEFT TO MURDER (Book #5)
LEFT TO ENVY (Book #6)
LEFT TO LAPSE (Book #7)

THE AU PAIR SERIES
ALMOST GONE (Book#1)
ALMOST LOST (Book #2)
ALMOST DEAD (Book #3)

ZOE PRIME MYSTERY SERIES
FACE OF DEATH (Book#1)
FACE OF MURDER (Book #2)
FACE OF FEAR (Book #3)
FACE OF MADNESS (Book #4)
FACE OF FURY (Book #5)
FACE OF DARKNESS (Book #6)

A JESSIE HUNT PSYCHOLOGICAL SUSPENSE SERIES
THE PERFECT WIFE (Book #1)

THE PERFECT BLOCK (Book #2)
THE PERFECT HOUSE (Book #3)
THE PERFECT SMILE (Book #4)
THE PERFECT LIE (Book #5)
THE PERFECT LOOK (Book #6)
THE PERFECT AFFAIR (Book #7)
THE PERFECT ALIBI (Book #8)
THE PERFECT NEIGHBOR (Book #9)
THE PERFECT DISGUISE (Book #10)
THE PERFECT SECRET (Book #11)
THE PERFECT FAÇADE (Book #12)
THE PERFECT IMPRESSION (Book #13)
THE PERFECT DECEIT (Book #14)
THE PERFECT MISTRESS (Book #15)

CHLOE FINE PSYCHOLOGICAL SUSPENSE SERIES
NEXT DOOR (Book #1)
A NEIGHBOR'S LIE (Book #2)
CUL DE SAC (Book #3)
SILENT NEIGHBOR (Book #4)
HOMECOMING (Book #5)
TINTED WINDOWS (Book #6)

KATE WISE MYSTERY SERIES
IF SHE KNEW (Book #1)
IF SHE SAW (Book #2)
IF SHE RAN (Book #3)
IF SHE HID (Book #4)
IF SHE FLED (Book #5)
IF SHE FEARED (Book #6)
IF SHE HEARD (Book #7)

THE MAKING OF RILEY PAIGE SERIES
WATCHING (Book #1)
WAITING (Book #2)
LURING (Book #3)
TAKING (Book #4)
STALKING (Book #5)
KILLING (Book #6)

CAUSE TO SAVE (Book #5)
CAUSE TO DREAD (Book #6)

KERI LOCKE MYSTERY SERIES
A TRACE OF DEATH (Book #1)
A TRACE OF MUDER (Book #2)
A TRACE OF VICE (Book #3)
A TRACE OF CRIME (Book #4)
A TRACE OF HOPE (Book #5)

Made in the USA
Columbia, SC
10 September 2021